1

TAGGIE

Tonight, I'm like Sleeping Beauty. One kiss, and I'm outta here.

Get my first kiss, then leave this bramble-infested—fine they're people, but they scratch at me like brambles—place forever. Night clubs are not my thing.

Also like Sleeping Beauty, I've accepted the first man who comes along. Is this guy a prince? Euuhhh... I'm not asking questions. Enthusiasm has to count for something, right? And Lance—I think that's his name anyway, the club was loud—is very enthusiastic.

I really thought I'd lose my k-card to an older man. There's even someone I've seen around a few times who would be my dream first kiss. But it's Friday night, and while I couldn't find any of the girls from my university course who said they'd be here, blond and nice Lance with his big smile and dull small talk approached me at the bar, and he's... Okay.

We couldn't really converse much over the music, so when he suggested we go somewhere quieter, I thought why not? A girl has to live her life and get rid of her first kiss sometime, and before turning twenty-one would be good.

"You don't mind if my brothers join us," Lance says, and it's not quite a question as two other young men catch up with us as we step out into the street. I shiver and tug down the skirt of my not-particularly short dress, because it's dark and chilly, the late Spring evening turning cold.

"Hi." I glance at Lance's brothers. They look similar to him. Lanky, blond, wearing deck shoes with no socks, chinos, and pale pastel-coloured shirts. "You're coming with us to the pub?"

Not much chance of talking or kissing with the four of us. Despite their posh and harmless appearance, chilled water slides down my spine as I look into their dark-blue eyes.

"Hey Agatha," says the chubbier one, giving me a thin-lipped smile.

I bristle. Not only did Lance somehow text his brothers, he told them to call me Agatha? My full name the way he says it makes me sound like I'm a virgin old lady with a crochet teapot cover and a yappy little dog.

And twenty-one is *not* old, and I don't have any pets. Yet.

"Taggie," I correct him. "Everyone calls me Taggie."

"Sure, Agatha," he sneers.

What am I doing? This isn't me. Even though an older man has made me inexplicably horny with his mere presence, this isn't what I want. I've never been into guys my own age.

"Shut up, Boris," says the other brother.

We're at the corner of a dark side street, and you know, maybe I'm done for this evening. Perhaps I'm not sleeping beauty. No kiss for me.

ABDUCTED BY THE MAFIA DON

EVIE ROSE

I stop walking.

"I think I might just call it a night." I feign a yawn. "You go on. I'll get a taxi."

"Ahh don't be a spoilsport," says Lance, hooking his arm through mine with a surprisingly tight grip and pulling me around, down the alleyway.

"Yeah," chimes in Boris, wrapping his arm over my shoulder in an over-friendly manner that simultaneously makes my skin crawl and traps me from bolting away. "The night is young. Don't leave us yet."

"The pub isn't this way." My voice comes out high and frightened. "Where are we going?"

"George knows a fun *shortcut*, don't you, George," replies Boris, and they all laugh.

"I certainly do," George replies, and there's something in the words that really scares me.

I try to pull away, but they hold me tighter, almost dragging me along into the deserted street, the tarmac wet beneath my scraping feet.

"Come on, you knew what you were getting into," Lance says with a sickly smile.

"I didn't!" I bleat. "I just thought we'd go to the pub."

"You sluts want more than that." George grabs his crotch meaningfully, angling it at me, and their laughter is loud and cruel.

Mad, animal panic overtakes me, and I throw myself around and down, escaping the only thing in my head now. That and terror. I get under Boris' arm, but Lance's fingers bite into my wrist, sending crippling pain all the way up to my shoulder.

"Oh no you don't." Boris grabs me up by my hair, and I scream as they shove me against the brick wall, knocking the breath out of me. The rough surface tears at my skin.

I fight. I kick and slap, but there are three of them, and they're still men, even though they're not brawny. I'm thrashing, but there's nothing I can do.

Fear courses through me painfully. Not the good sort of pain. The sharp, jagged kind that shrivels and dries and cracks. I'm brittle, and crying, shouting incoherently and kicking out.

Within seconds I'm on the ground, all four of my limbs held, the backs of my bare legs in the grit of the tarmac.

Desperately, I look up and down the alleyway. No one is coming. I'm alone.

"Little whore is a fighter," George says, eyes gleaming. He pulls a knife from his back pocket and the blade mirrors the sickly orange street-light and his pink shirt.

"I'm not a whore," I whisper. I'm trembling, and my voice is stronger than I expect. "I've never even been kissed." Maybe I can get them to feel sorry for me.

"She's never been kissed, boys," Lance sneers. "Virgin too, like a proper Essex girl. Stupid bitch is going to get us all smeared in blood by the end of the night."

They all chuckle.

Tears seep from my eyes.

I'm such an idiot. I should have known this would go bad.

"Let's have a look at you..." George says, pressing the blade to my breast.

"Please don't," I sob out.

George rolls his eyes and the strap of my dress slices through. He grabs the swell of it, and I recoil.

"No. No. Help!" I shout, but I know no one is going to. I don't even have a dad who would avenge or get angry about what's about to happen. It's just me and my grandmother.

"No, no, don't," Boris mimics as he shoves my hips painfully down, and rips my skirt up.

"Let me go. No!"

"Hold her," says Lance. "Shut up you stupid bitch, or it'll be less important that you get to our father in one piece."

I scream louder, because he'll be worse. The father will be worse.

"Get her gag, Boris." He's undoing his trousers. "And open her legs. I'm having my due—"

"Stop." The deep voice of a man cuts through the chaos.

George glances over his shoulder with a sneer. "Mind your own business."

A terrified noise continues to come from my mouth. They don't let go.

"Touch her and die." The dark menace of the man in the shadow's statement reverberates through me despite everything. He's all causal power, and I'm silenced by it somehow.

Like this man could tell the earth to stop spinning, and it would.

My assailants don't feel the same.

Lance snorts, and turns back to me, taking his pasty, skinny length in hand. It's the first time I've ever seen this part of a man, and even through my terror, I'm not impressed.

Women get excited about *that*?

The noise is subtle. The release from my leg doesn't register initially, only the spray of warm liquid.

"Shit!" Then a gurgle, and Boris slumps on top of me.

Another splatter of blood.

Then I look up in shock. The impossibly tall man, in a

black suit, his face in shadow, is gazing down at me. The thick barrel of a silencer gleams.

My scream dies in my throat.

The man puts the gun away with an elegant flick of his hand then strides over, black polished leather shoes crunching on the tarmac.

"Sorry about that," he says in a low voice. His tone is polite and refined. With one foot, he rolls Boris' lifeless body off me.

I'm shaking and tears are pouring from my wide-open eyes. It's cold, yes. A spring night, and my dress is torn. But it's the panic receding that causes my shivers.

The warm spots of moisture turn cool. I'm covered with their blood.

"Here." The man strips off his suit jacket, and I get no more than a moment of the scent of sage and cedarwood and a flicker of a cheekbone as he kneels.

Then he offers his hand, and his white shirt pulls up to reveal a solid and expensive-looking watch, gold cufflinks, and a jagged tattoo that snakes over the back of his hand. He turns his palm upwards and waits.

Another sob escapes me, and for a second, I consider refusing. After all, I trusted one man—well, boy—tonight, and that turned out to be an error. I should have listened to my grandmother. She always says men are trouble. That's why she won't tell me anything about my father. Secretly, I've longed for a dad, or a man I could trust. And kiss.

And that was an awful mistake.

But this feels different.

I peek up at my saviour, and although his face is in shadow, a little of the confidence I began the evening with and have felt for the last week, trickles back.

I take his hand and allow him to help me to sit up.

"Good girl," he rumbles. "Did they hurt you?" He drapes his jacket over my shoulders, covering me with his warmth, and the rich scent of him. Something green and earthy and masculine.

I make a noise to object. Maybe I use words?

"Blood, jacket, I—"

The man shushes me and shakes his head, pulling the jacket tighter, the silky-soft interior comforting on my skin.

"You're safe. No one will ever harm you again." He has a rumbling voice that's so reassuring. "What's your name?"

"Taggie. Agatha Hayes, but everyone calls me Taggie," I stammer, but not because I'm scared now. I'm... The relief coursing through me is a river of sugar and wine. Heady.

"I'm sorry this happened to you, Taggie," he murmurs.

"Who are you?" My voice is weak, and my throat is sore.

"Their father's enemy," he says quietly as he slides his arm around my back and under my knees, lifting me.

Enemy? I squeak and grasp for his shirt, but he has me held tight. Not the bad sort of earlier, though. Nope. A warm, secure kind of hold, and I let my palm rest over his hard pectoral muscle.

"You're coming with me."

Probably I should fight or scream, or at least make a snarky comment. But he just shot three men who were trying to hurt me, so I'm giving this stranger leeway. Besides, his jacket smells delicious, and he's warm and solid.

I relax into him as he carries me out of the alley, and only a few steps into the street to a sleek black limousine.

In the glow of the interior light as he lifts me inside, I finally get a good look at the man who has saved me, and jolt. He looked tall and broad and intimidating as he appeared like an avenging hero, but now I can see more details.

He's older. He has black hair with a slight wave, and it's shot through with silver that glints. His square jaw is hard-set and covered with black stubble. There's a scar that runs down next to his ear.

And he has a pair of brown eyes so dark they're almost black, with faint lines radiating out that reveal he's probably twice my age.

Familiar eyes. Eyes I would never forget if I'd seen them once, but it hasn't been once.

No. I've seen these tummy-fluttering fathomless eyes before. They've followed me around for the last week. They're the reason I've been feeling restless, and like I want my first kiss.

"What's your name?" I ask with a gulp. And I'm afraid again, but a different sort of fear, that's thrilling. Things are clicking into place.

"Dominic Richmond," he says calmly.

This is insane.

I think the most dangerous mafia boss in London has been stalking me.

2

DOM

It's a good thing I've been following my girl. Fuck. That was far too close, and it's a sign. She's not leaving me again.

I was her stalker, but now she'll have to be my captive.

Her eyes widen. She recognises my name.

This is exactly what I was trying to avoid. Scaring her. My gorgeous little doll. Mia bambola.

I suppose this was inevitable. The price of my revenge against the man who killed my parents and siblings.

I slide in beside her in the armoured limo, and help her with her seat belt as we speed away. My driver knows where to take us. Out of the centre of London and back to the leafy comfort of Richmond.

The daughter of the man I live to torture is more beautiful up close, and in my arms, than I realised. Even covered in blood. Taggie's curly blonde hair is messed up, and she's flushed. Still recovering from her ordeal with those stupid boys I was saving to die later, when Thaxted was more attached to his newfound sons.

But Taggie is more important than my plans.

"Dominic Richmond," she repeats softly, and my name on her lips is heaven.

"You can call me Dom, though. Nobody else does." Not anymore.

"Dom."

"Yeah." God, but that feels good. I've never thought of it before, but the way she says "Dom" with her little pink mouth, as though it's something sacred, makes me think how I'd like her to be my submissive, and to be her Dominant. Take care of her and have her obey.

She'd be beautiful.

"Where are we going, Dom?" she whispers.

"Somewhere you'll be safe." With me. She's mine now. "To my house."

I wait to see if she'll shrink away, but she doesn't, and my heart pulses.

I love seeing her wrapped in my jacket. It's absurdly oversized, but just right. From the moment I saw her, I knew. I had a feeling. The sort that as a person who relies on spine tingles to keep me alive, I've learned not to ignore.

This isn't what I planned to do with my enemy's daughter, but Taggie has rewritten every rule. All the things I thought were important are dust.

"Thank you." She looks across at me, and despite the blood spots on her, I'm struck again by how beautiful she is. Her bottom lip trembles. "If you hadn't found me..."

"I did though." *I'll always find you. I'll always protect you. You're mine.*

Those words are too much right now, so I don't say them, but they're a promise nonetheless.

"I should go home. My granny will be worried about me."

"You'll worry her a lot more if you go home like that." I

indicate her blood-stained clothes. "You can clean up at my place." I sort of infer that she can leave after that.

Looking down at her ripped dress seems to enhance the echo of what nearly just happened and she's shaking again when we pull up at the glossy black front door of the house the Richmonds have lived in for generations. It's a huge, white-painted Georgian mansion, with classic twelve-paned windows and views over the river and Richmond Park. It's a house meant for a massive, extended family to live and work together in.

Now it's just me, a lonely metal ball rolling around.

"Oh! You don't have to..." she exclaims as I pick her up and carry her inside.

"Don." My head of household is immediately at my side, sounding shaken.

"A glass of water, bar of chocolate, antiseptic—" I bark.

"I'm fine!" Taggie tries to interrupt.

I rattle off the other items I need and Edward replies with a prompt, "Yes, Don."

In the lounge, I set her on a plush deep-green velvet sofa.

"I'll get blood stains all over..." she protests and immediately goes to stand.

Kneeling before her, I give her a gentle push back on her shoulder. "It'll be cleaned."

She looks up at me, and I stroke her arm through the dark fabric, as though this a casual thing for me, and withdraw.

The connection between us hums. She's so sweet, so vulnerable, but she's brave. I saw her kicking the Thaxted boys, and I'm sure she'd do the same to me if I overstepped.

"You really don't have to go to all this trouble," she murmurs, but sinks back down.

I shake my head. She has no idea what I will do for her. "Show me."

Blinking uncertainly, she slides my jacket off, and I hiss out a breath. There's the beginning of pink bruising on her upper arm.

"I thought..." She twists to examine it. "It hurt, but it doesn't now."

There's blood, and when Edward sets down the items I requested beside me, I immediately start wiping it away. The tense feeling in my chest eases a little each time smooth, unbroken skin is revealed.

I clean right down to her fingertips, and she allows me, watching as though she can't believe it.

When she's perfect again there, I gesture for her to lean forwards, and check her back. There's nothing there, and I sigh with relief then move to her feet, trying not to notice too much of the delectable parts of her between.

Her strappy shoes are made for partying not walking, and my big hands envelop her whole foot easily. It's not until the backs of her calves, and just above her knees, that I find scratches.

Anger rises in me hot as lava.

"Really, the pain is gone," she assures me.

I have to unclench my jaw with physical effort so I can reply, "I'm glad."

I touch her knee, and Taggie parts her thighs for me before I've even asked, and the air goes thick and scalding in my throat. I can't breathe for how perfect she is.

Watching her face the whole time, I gently wash away every trace of their blood and their touch. A purification. I'm careful not to touch anywhere inappropriate, and I'm intent on making sure she's okay.

It's not sexual, though my cock can't help but respond to

her proximity. There's more joy and closeness in taking care of Taggie as she deserves than I've felt in any of the one-night stands I've had.

Drawing the skirt of her dress down, I sit on my heels, clear up, then nudge her glass of water and plate of sweet treats closer to her hand and stand.

"Thank you."

When I turn back to her, she's looking up at me, and I know how the sun must feel gazing down on a single, perfect sunflower. I'm this fiery dangerous far-off angry ball of exploding reactions, and she's a delicate thing that would be burned to charred remains if she comes too close. But the way she tilts herself towards the threat makes me want to protect her even more.

The daughter of Thaxted.

It's almost Shakespearian. My only love sprung from my only hate.

"You're welcome." I'm hoarse with emotion. "It's late. You should call your grandmother, but I insist you stay the night."

"I couldn't, I'll get a taxi—"

"I *insist*." My voice drops to a rough growl.

She presses her lips together, and nods.

My poor body is tensing and relaxing like this is a fucking stress test for a lump of steel. Which to be honest, is the current status for my shoulders, spine, and cock. I gesture for her to go ahead of me, and direct her up the grand main staircase to the upper floor.

"I hope this will be comfortable for you." I shove the door open, revealing a bedroom, with adjoining library, sitting room, and ensuite bathroom through arched doorways. "All the connecting rooms are for your use. Feel free to look around."

Her intake of breath is gratifying as she takes it in.

Every detail was hacked and stolen from her life. I am a monstrous bowerbird, making a perfectly decorated nest for my female, hoping to lure her in.

I told myself it was to understand her better, but it wasn't. It was in the hope of that reaction. Delight.

Though the inevitable questions will be less welcome, and I have the perfect excuse for not answering them now.

"Sleep well. One more thing." The temptation of her nearby is too much for my threadbare control. "Lock your door."

She blinks at me in shock.

"If you need to feel safer," I add, trying to sound reasonable. "You've been through a lot. Barricade it if necessary. But I guarantee you are safe in this house."

"Okay." She nods.

"You understand?" I repeat. "Lock the door."

3

TAGGIE

I look up into his face, and the scars and his fathomless dark eyes are beautiful in a way I can't explain.

"Yes. I understand." But I don't.

"Good." He turns abruptly, strides down the hallway and takes the stairs two at a time. Like he can't wait to get away from me.

I squash the feeling of disappointment, because for an evening that was a nightmare, it's really done a switch.

How did I get so lucky? I've fallen into a dream.

This room is unbelievable.

Sometimes people say that about a cake, or a pair of jeans, or a news story. But those things aren't unbelievable. They're usually exactly what you'd expect.

But this... No. I can hardly trust my eyes. There's no explanation.

It really is baffling.

The kingpin of Richmond has a suite of rooms—not just one room, oh no—that are stuffed full of everything I've ever wished for. It's almost as big as the house I share with Granny.

I recognise the rug from something I pinned on social media. The acres of bookshelves hold the contents of my online wish list. The curtains are the fabric I admired on a website last week, and the bed covers are from a shop I browsed in just two days ago.

Several laps aren't enough, I can't stop.

There's a mini-library, with shelves in a deep-blue that reach floor to ceiling, and there's a ladder. With wheels. I give it an experimental push, and it glides over the wooden floor perfectly. I step onto it, and climb right to the top, where there are pretty, hardback editions of classics. Lower down, there are rows of fantasy romance paperbacks, and at the bottom, reference books and key psychology texts that I've been reading for university. Stepping back down, I leave my foot on the bottom rung. A little shove and the ladder rolls across, and I'm grinning like a loon as I do it again.

This is... Look, it's so good it's definitely an illusion. But I'm obsessed with it.

I slip books off the shelf and run my fingers over cushions. There's a perfect little reading sofa that I liked a post of something similar recently.

There are three missed calls and four messages from my grandmother when I pull out my phone. It went into "sleep" mode hours ago, which I suppose was considerate of it. Letting me party—and be sort of kidnapped—uninterrupted.

"Taggie, where are you?" Granny answers on my second ring.

"Safe," I tell her. "Everything is fine. I've ended up..." I consider how to phrase this in a way that won't make her worry. "Going back to someone's house."

I cross my fingers behind my back, even though there's no one to see.

"Who is he?" Granny asks after a beat of silence.

Uh. She'll flip out if I say he's a mafia boss twice my age. And it doesn't matter, as I'll be home tomorrow, I acknowledge with a pang of regret. I glance around the room that has all my favourite things, and think of the man I've just met, who feels so familiar I'm really wondering if he were deliberately following me.

Absurd.

So I confess the simplest part of the story. "I was having a bit of trouble at the club—"

"What sort?" she interrupts me. "Was it the Essex cartel?"

"It was just some guys, I'm not sure who they were exactly." Essex is a bogeyman in London, and Granny has always been bordering on paranoid about the mafias. I don't want my ageing grandmother to freak out, given I'm perfectly safe now. "And this other man came to my rescue."

"A stranger?" she demands.

"I've seen him around." I press my crossed fingers tighter together.

"That's fine." She sounds relieved. "Someone from university then, and it's late. You should stay."

I'm grinning before she's finished the sentence, and kicking my feet with glee. I get to spend the night in this amazing bedroom, and play at the idea a hot, older man wants me! Whoever said reality was better than fiction doesn't have as vivid an imagination as me, and so much to feed it.

A squeal of excitement must escape me, as Granny laughs.

"Someone is happy," she comments.

"I like him," I admit impulsively, thinking of Dom. My dark saviour. The man who cleaned me up with such deliberate care. Who shot three men for me without a second thought.

"Well." I hear a smile in her voice now. "I take it you're calling me to tell me you won't be home tonight. Have a lovely time."

Ooff. My reality is getting further and further from this white lie I'm telling.

"Thanks," I say, hiding how pathetic I feel. "Good night."

We hang up, and I look around the room again. I wonder who it's for? A girl with more courage than me, that's certain.

On impulse, I search online for Dominic Richmond. There's no mention of a girlfriend, or daughter. But I remembered correctly—he's hard and dangerous. His whole family was killed in a mafia dispute with an Essex Cartel member, and Dom "miraculously" was the only one who survived, and "conveniently" took over his family's mafia. There's a lot of scepticism about the timing of those circumstances.

Whatever he did in the past, today he saved me. I look for a long time at a photograph of Dom at one of the London social events. He's wearing a tux and appears as handsome and serious as when I've seen him in the last week. Following me? I still can't believe that.

There's something wrong with me that it doesn't put me off him that I saw him kill three men, and that he might have been complicit in his family's murders. I'm oddly certain I'm safe with him, despite his clear lack of ethics.

He told me to lock my bedroom door so I feel secure.

In an instant, I've made a decision. I'm at the door, and I've turned the key, unlocking it.

Despite what happened tonight, I'm determined to be brave.

I don't need to feel *safer* in Dom's house. He's a tiger, and I want to run my hands through his fur, have his paws maul me, feel his sharp teeth on my neck. I like that he's dangerous, and all that banked power as he crouched at my feet, ready to pounce.

There are some clothes left out, and I have a shower and then put them on. The bed is perfectly comfortable, and as soon as my head hits the pillow, I'm dreaming.

Dom

Pining. I'm fucking pining for this girl. Saving her, speaking with her, has only convinced me more that she's a perfect match for me. And she's a world away, safely behind a locked door.

That should satisfy me. She's in my house, and no one can harm her.

So why do I want more? Why do crave forbidden, unspeakable things? She's been through enough tonight without discovering that I'm obsessed with her.

I tell myself I'm going downstairs to make a cup of something to help me sleep. And I do. But I drink it in the kitchen, and trudge back upstairs with longing in my heavy heart.

I just need a reminder of the limits. All that's required is to be clear why she's not for me. A nudge that says, *this girl cannot be yours tonight or ever.* She's too young, innocent, and good for a man like me.

Feeling the resistance of her locked door, the evidence of her fear, will do it.

I make silent footsteps to Taggie's suite and stop before her bedroom door. She's scared, I tell myself. She locked her door because I told her to if she needed to feel safe. This will be the evidence I need that I have to keep my distance.

I reach out and grasp the handle. Turning it... and... The door swings open.

Oh. Shit.

I am a good enough man to stay away from a frightened girl. I know I am. A girl who locked her door to protect herself.

But a brave girl who left her door open to me?

God help her. I cannot resist.

Taggie

In the dream, I'm reading a big hardback book. The story is about... I don't know. The pages are turning too fast. I can't read it.

"Taggie," a man's voice says. "Taggie."

The pages turn faster and faster, the rub of them frantic.

"You're so beautiful. I can't help it. I want you so much."

The pages flick, but they're wet. It sounds wet now, like the paper is slick.

A low groan vibrates through me, coming from the book.

I open my eyes, and in the darkness, I could swear I see the silhouette of a man, standing over me, black eyes glistening like onyx.

I blink.

And then he's gone, a dream. And my eyelids are heavy, so I drift back into sleep.

4

DOM

"Don." My second-in-command opens my office door and hesitates. "I found the girl—"

I jolt as I see Taggie behind him, wearing an oversized T-shirt and a pair of baggy leggings with seemingly nothing else. Her curly hair is tousled and a bit fluffy, like a blonde halo.

It's barely seven in the morning. I thought she'd sleep for hours more.

Her gaze zeroes in on me as though we're connected, and I have to suppress a jolt as I remember standing over her in the darkness last night, fisting my cock until I came with a low groan of hollow satisfaction.

Just being near her was a turn-on, and it is now too.

"Come in, bambola." I can't stop looking at my girl as she creeps forwards.

Most people's eyes are drawn straight to the row of windows behind me that look out onto the River Thames and parkland on the other side. Taggie just looks at me.

"Thank you for bringing her to me, Gavino. That will be all."

Gavino nods, his brow furrowed with worry, but retreats silently.

"He calls you Dom?" She seems almost upset.

For a beat, I stare at her in a clash of confusion and lust. It must show on my face, since she mutters, "I thought you said no one called you that."

I smile at the misunderstanding. "No, he calls me the *Don*."

Gesturing at the chair in front of my desk, I retreat back to a safe distance where she can't see my erection pressing towards her, and nervously, she slides into the leather seat.

"Half my men are Italian, including Gavino. They came with my mother from Sardinia. The others are from London, like Edward who you met yesterday, and are my father's legacy. And they all call me Don, because..." I swallow. It's still a bit painful even after all this time. "Because that was what they called my father. He insisted on it as a mark of respect for my mother's heritage. We speak Italian for business a lot, and amongst the family, when..." I peter out, suddenly aware I've said more than I needed to. I can't help it. I want her to know everything, and have her feel at home in Richmond. It's a fucking stupid impulse. "I didn't mean to give you a whole history lesson."

Her eyes brighten. "It's okay."

A girl as lovely and innocent as Taggie isn't meant for a blood-soaked kingpin like me.

What would she say when I reveal that I've been stalking her since I first saw her? There would be the inevitable question of why I found her originally, and the answer to that is simple and unforgivable.

I intended to kill her.

And the moment I saw Taggie, everything changed. It's

not that I didn't believe in love. My parents loved each other, and my family cared about each other.

I just didn't think it was something that would happen to *me*.

I certainly didn't imagine I'd be fucking Romeo and Juliet'ed like a cliché from a 1990s movie. My only love sprung from my only hate.

She's Thaxted's *daughter*, but I can't murder her. I'd burn the world down before allowing anything to so much as bruise her.

"I just wanted to say thank you before I left." Taggie interrupts my thoughts with nervous words that pour out over each other too fast.

Something dark seeps into me. "You're welcome. But you need to stay long enough for the clothes I ordered to arrive. Charming though that look is..." I indicate the T-shirt that hangs almost to her knees. "Shoes, at least?"

"Oh." She wriggles uncomfortably. "I couldn't put you out like that."

"Nonsense. Sit. Some breakfast?" I quickly message Edward, requesting tea and hot buttered toast, and make a little show of asking what she wants and how she prefers her tea, as though I didn't already know she likes it white as her innocent soul, and just as sweet. Two teaspoonfuls of sugar.

"Did you sleep alright?" I say casually, and my heart jumps as a wary expression I can't identify flashes across her face.

"Yeah. No nightmares," she replies.

"Good." I ask her about her grandmother's reaction, and it doesn't take much prompting for her to tell me all about her granny. I gobble up every detail she unwittingly tells me about herself, from the fact that her grandmother thinks she reads too many books, and was sceptical about Taggie's psychology course at university, but Taggie won her round.

The tea and toast arrives and she cautiously takes a bite, then another as she finds it's exactly the bread she likes, slathered in butter.

"It's just you and your Grandmother?" A gentle probe. I'd listen to details of Taggie's life all day, but I need to be certain of the situation. How much danger is she really in?

"Yeah." She nods easily.

"And your mother?"

"We think she died when I was a baby. She disappeared, and apparently that wasn't like her."

"I'm sorry." I make a note to follow up and see if I can discover what happened.

"It's always been me and Granny, so it's been okay. I miss that I don't have a father more, to be honest." There's longing in her blue eyes as they meet mine. "I would try to find him, if I could."

I nod, in what I hope is a sympathetic way. She wants a father, would a Daddy do? I could manage that, but I'm not telling her she's the daughter of Thaxted.

"You don't know who he is?"

"No." The sadness around her eyes deepens. "Unknown on the birth certificate."

"Must be tough not to know your family." As painful as it is to have lost mine, I can't imagine the lonely gap not ever having them would leave.

She shrugs. "Granny says he was a waste of space."

That we can agree on. And thankfully, Taggie doesn't seem to know about Thaxted and his strategy of collecting his children at age twenty-one. That makes protecting her a little easier.

"The young men who attempted to assault you last night. Did you recognise them?" I check.

She shakes her head. "I'd never seen them before." Her gaze flicks up to mine, and I wonder for a second if she's going to add, "unlike you". But she doesn't. "I met them in the club, and one of them invited me to go to another bar with him."

Jealous fury flares in me.

He made a move on my girl. Little shit deserved to die for what he did to Taggie, but I might have murdered him for thinking he could even look at something so beautiful.

"Who were they...?" she asks tentatively.

"They're sons of Thaxted."

She shrugs and gives me a blank look.

"He's the kingpin of Thaxted in Essex. Part of the Essex cartel."

That makes her draw in a breath, and I know by the flash of fear in her eyes that she understands my meaning.

London mafia bosses are feared and loved in equal measure. The Essex cartel? They're just hated.

"So," she pauses. "Why is he your enemy?"

She's remarkably direct for a slight little thing. I do her the honour of responding in the same way.

"Because two years ago he killed my whole family in cold blood," I say simply, but there's nothing simple about it.

The Richmond mafia was a happy, corrupt family that argued and loved and cared for each other.

We weren't unreasonable. We made huge amounts of money, my father was the sort of mafia don who knew every person who worked for him by name, and the shouting matches were as passionate as the Italian heritage on my mother's side would have you believe.

The funeral brought the whole of Richmond to a stand-still for two days as people came to pay their respects.

"This was retaliation?" She peeks at me from under her long lashes, her curls over her cheeks as though she's trying to hide her thoughts, but I read them anyway.

"Yes," I reply. "But I can see that you think perhaps after two years I don't really care?"

"No!" she squawks, and it's obviously a "yes".

"There's a rumour that I collaborated with Thaxted to have my family killed so I could inherit."

I encouraged the whispers, and evidently, they reached Taggie. They work in my favour, inflating my already brutal nature to legendary coldness and danger.

And it has the bonus of working for deceiving Thaxted, too. My spy in the heart of Thaxted's family tells me that he believes I'm indifferent to the fact he murdered what he thinks was my competition in acquiring power.

Taggie makes a small sound like "err" from the back of her throat and won't meet my eyes.

"It's not true. I was the eldest son, and would have inherited anyway."

She bites her lip and toys uncertainly with the hem of her T-shirt. She doesn't believe me, and I can feel her slipping through my fingers as she judges me as unfeeling.

"I love my family."

"Of course you do," she replies quickly. "Did."

"Do. And I can prove it." I shouldn't say this. I haven't told anyone my plan.

That gets her attention. She gazes over at me, her navy eyes full of curiosity.

"Come here."

Shyly, she rises and creeps around and at the sight of

her gorgeous body hidden by my baggy T-shirt, I remember why I decided she should remain on the other side of my desk. She's temptation incarnate, and my cock throbs with need.

But she's here now. I adjust myself as I lean forwards, moving her attention to my computer. Obediently, she looks, and draws in a shocked breath.

The background on the monitor is a family picture.

"It was taken three Christmases ago. That's Lorenzo, and Giovanni." I point them out. "That's my mother, and my father. My youngest sister, Isabella. My elder sister, Serena."

"You all look so happy," she says after a second, sounding wistful.

"We were."

She twitches towards me, as though to come to comfort me. "I'm so sorry."

"Thank you."

"What happened?"

"I think now it was because of a deal my father wouldn't agree to." A trafficking deal. One of the few things we all agreed on. I wave my hand, because it's best not to get into the disgusting details. "I suspect we pricked his pride, and he didn't forget. It all seemed fine, and everything went on as usual. Then one of Thaxted's sons became close with my little sister, and she fell in love. He proposed."

I shrug, as though this part of the story doesn't hurt more than any other. I'd brought the wrath of my whole family by insisting this was a bad idea. Isabella had been furious with me.

"My family went to Thaxted in force, to consider the proposal. He poisoned them all at the engagement dinner. I wasn't there."

"Why not?" she asks, then bites her lip as though she regrets the question.

"I disagreed with the marriage and refused to attend. Instead, I was at a meeting of the then newly-formed London Mafia Syndicate."

Her eyes are full of sympathy I'm not sure I deserve with hands as covered in blood as mine are.

"With the help of the London Mafia Syndicate, I took over, and rebuilt. Richmond is stronger now than ever."

She eyes me. "But you keep that photo on your computer where only you'll see it? You could have a portrait on the wall and everyone would know—"

"It suits my purpose to have Thaxted and others believe that I don't care that he murdered my family."

"Why?" she asks, brow furrowed. "And why wait so long to kill all of Thaxted's sons?"

Cute that she thinks he only has three sons, and I haven't killed the others yet. Thaxted has only one child alive at this point, out of the many he had. Admittedly, he thinks he has two.

My spy—Harrison—is pretending to be Thaxted's son. Like a cuckoo laying its eggs in the nest of another bird, Thaxted is pouring his resources into Harrison, unaware that I murdered his real son. And Thaxted has become attached to my spy, which will make it all the sweeter when Harrison betrays him.

"Oh. You killed the others already." Her eyes widen.

"Such a clever girl." I smile slightly at the way she has put the pieces of the puzzle together.

She pulls herself up a bit straighter at my praise. "If it were me, I'd want revenge."

"I do." I pause, because my throat feels rusty with disuse on this subject. "I keep the photo there because it helps me remember why I breathe every day. My mother was deeply superstitious. I wasn't there, but I have reports that corroborate what I know in my gut. Before she died, she cursed Thaxted."

She nods, as though this is a totally sane thing to do.

"And that curse? It's *me*."

5

DOM

"You?" she echoes, leaning back against the edge of my desk.

An unknowing temptation. I'd love to push her onto the glossy dark wood and shove myself between her thighs, my hand over her mouth.

"I am the curse my mother put on Thaxted."

"I don't get it." She tilts her head to the side, reminding me of an adorably confused puppy.

"One of the things Thaxted and Richmond had, or maybe have, in common was a belief in the importance of legacy." As I say the words, there's a slam of realisation.

Her.

Taggie is supposed to be part of *Richmond*. She's the one who should have my children and means that Richmond has a new generation of raucous family.

I push the revelation aside. It can't be.

"Thaxted also believes intensely in tradition and family. But his method is different. Instead of a loving, connected group with children growing up with their parents, he's of the 'introduce me to my sons when they're twenty-one' philosophy."

I don't mention daughters. I don't want her to make this connection. But her brow is furrowed with lack of understanding about where this is going, so I think I'm fine.

"He has dozens of children, and unlike Richmond, which my parents made a tight family unit, he only cares about them when they're old enough to be useful to him."

Her lip wrinkles.

"Exactly," I agree with her implicit assessment. "He killed my family, so I carry out my mother's curse and take from him what he cares about most: his family tradition.

"Since he murdered my family, he has become exceptionally unlucky. His eldest son died in a car accident. His next eldest died because of faulty electrical wiring in his house. The others had a house fire, drug overdose caused by a bad batch, blood poisoning during a routine operation, severe allergic reaction causing hospitalisation and subsequently dying of a secondary infection, an accident when cleaning a gun that was loaded, and a fall down the stairs. Every common, unfortunate cause of death has been visited on Thaxted's family since he killed the Richmond mafia."

The corners of her mouth tug upwards. "You're the curse."

"But you can call me Dom." I keep my face blank.

She giggles and we're gazing at each other, and the connection is as intense as it is undeniable.

It takes a long moment, then her expression freezes.

"And that's why you were there that night."

Or alternatively, I was following her because I need her close by so I can breathe. I've fallen in passionate and tragic love with a girl half my age who was supposed to be part of my vengeance.

"Mm." I make a sound that could be agreement. "The thing is, I moved on them earlier than I planned."

"Oh." Her face falls. "I'm sorry."

"Don't be. I'm not."

"Being shot in the head isn't really part of the 'cursed' plan," she says with a snort.

I shrug. "This is London, and those bullies were asking for trouble. It could have been anyone who killed them."

But it wasn't, and I suspect Thaxted will realise that. It's too much of a coincidence that they were in London to retrieve Taggie and were all murdered together. Even if they were fucked-up little shits who were going against Essex rules to keep their sister a virgin.

"I should go," she says suddenly, and I'm not prepared.

"No." The word is harsh and out before I can stop it. "You're staying here."

Instead of being alarmed, as she ought to be, Taggie merely looks at me with a touch of confusion. "I can't do that."

"I think he might target you." Look, that sounds rational. Protective. Considerate, even. Not at all like I will hold her hostage and spoil her until she can't imagine leaving.

Her eyes fill with panic.

"I'd like you to remain here, for your own safety. Since his three sons are dead, I suspect he'll be looking for revenge, and you..." I leave it dangling, and she makes the connection.

"He'll think I killed them?!" Taggie's mouth falls open, and she's so genuinely horrified by the idea, I nearly laugh.

"No, but he's not known for proportional reactions," I say dryly, and neglect to mention that I'm not either.

"Oh. Right." She pinches her eyebrows together in sympathy. "Sorry."

"I couldn't protect my family, but I can protect you, Taggie," I tell her, low and earnestly, and in some ways honestly. I'm not above using every advantage I have. "But I need you close to ensure your safety."

That's a plausible reason that isn't that I'm hoping she might fall in love with me from mere proximity. Which is absurd, of course. My love for her won't transmit by osmosis.

More's the pity.

But maybe... Just maybe if she had to show me affection, a gentle bambola like Taggie would find it easier to think of a scarred, tattooed, morally repugnant man who is twice her age as more than what he is? If I planted the seed of the idea that we would be good together, perhaps it could grow?

She blinks. "Why would you help me? I don't understand."

"He'll discover soon enough that I murdered them, and he'll wonder *why*."

The baffled expression on her face is truly cute. "Because you found them intending to..."

Rape her. She can't say it.

"And if Thaxted can't get at me—which he can't—he'll come after the next best thing. The person he might hold responsible for his sons' deaths."

"Me," she whispers.

"And if it were just that I was rescuing a damsel in distress, he would think he can take out his anger without repercussion."

Taggie covers her mouth with her hands, horror in every angle of her slight body.

"It would be better if he thought you're important to me. Then he wouldn't dare touch you."

This is all the surface of a lie with the kernel of truth.

Thaxted *will* come after her, but because she's his daughter. She*'ll* be safer with me, because I'll protect her with not only my life, but the lives of every person I can get hold of. I'd build a house of human bones if that was the best way to defend Taggie.

"But I'm not." Her expression is a bit sad. "We only just met." She rakes her eyes—fuck they are her father's eyes—over my body from head to toes, as though I'm a half-forgotten dream. And even as I wonder if she saw me stalking her, I feel her regard like it's her hands. Sensation ripples down my spine then spreads through to my cock, which thickens.

Fuck it. There are only two options here: she knows she's my captive, or she accepts my offer.

"I could protect you properly if he thought you were my wife."

Her shock is almost a physical thing. I've never seen someone so still. It's like she thinks if she moves or draws breath that will change what I've just said.

"What if I had come to pick you up from that club because I was your husband?"

I can practically see her mind whirring. "I left with those boys, I couldn't have anyone thinking—"

"They wouldn't," I cut her off abruptly. "You went to the club to meet your friends from university, left a little early, and were grabbed while you waited for me to pick you up."

"I guess..." She's a bit breathless, and frankly so am I.

She hasn't said no yet. I can hardly believe my luck.

"So, what, we're engaged?"

"Married." I don't like the idea of an engagement. That could be broken off. "Have been for a year."

She huffs with laughter. "This is ridiculous, no one

would ever believe you married me. And how would they even know?"

"We'll go to some events, and tell everyone we kept our marriage a secret because your grandmother disapproved, and you didn't feel comfortable leaving her alone."

The sounds of doubt that come from her mouth would be endearing if I weren't wracked with nerves that I'll have to lock her in this house to keep her.

But she still doesn't say no.

"Just until the threat from Thaxted is over?" she checks. "And then, what? We'll pretend to divorce?"

No. Absolutely not.

I nod vaguely.

"We'll figure something out." Specifically, something that involves her staying with me forever. "For now, let's ensure you look the part. Come on." I hold out my hand and then swear internally as her gaze drops to it.

I keep forgetting she doesn't feel this connection that I do.

It's only a fraction of a second, and I'm already withdrawing my arm, pretending I didn't desperately want to hold her hand, when she dives forward and her little, soft fingertips brush my big scarred knuckles.

I lead her upstairs to her bedroom, and to the dressing table—one of the only pieces of my mother's furniture that remained in here during last week's redesign. She gasps as I open the box, revealing jewellery passed down through the Richmond family for generations.

"Choose any ring you like."

"I couldn't." She looks up at me, then down at the array of priceless heirloom jewels.

"Try."

"But they're all so beautiful and expensive."

I attempt to see it through her eyes. To me, there are hundreds of tiny memories of my mother and my grandmother and my sisters wearing the necklaces and brooches and rings. There's every type of combination of stones in shades of blue and green and purple—the colours of Richmond. Emeralds, amethysts, sapphires, and aquamarines. Big, showy rings and simple rows of princess-cut diamonds.

I guess it could seem intimidating.

"Taggie, my wife should have—"

"But I'm not your wife." She takes a step back, shying away, and I grit my teeth.

I really should have opted for a different strategy. Somehow, I imagined that if we pretended we'd been in love for a year already, the outward situation would match the way I feel inside: like I've been in love with Taggie forever.

My heart, of course, but also my lungs.

"Why are you doing this for me? I'm nobody."

She's everything to me. Now she's here in the same room, I can't imagine how I survived without her. It's as though she's an essential organ.

"You could think that I'm doing this to make up for what I couldn't do in the past," I suggest. That would be wrong, but you could.

It's the right thing to say. She relaxes, and when I gesture to the rings again, she steps forwards, and we pour over the tray together, me suggesting, pointing out larger diamonds and emeralds until she laughs and accepts the sparkliest one in white gold with sapphires and diamonds.

Sliding the ring onto her finger, and seeing her pleased smile, is magic.

"Call your grandmother and tell her I'm sending a car," I say to cover the fact I just want to kiss her.

"Oh, she'll never leave her house," Taggie replies, looking up from her ring. "No chance."

I scowl. I'd rather have everything under my control.

"Ask her anyway. Impress on her how important this is."

"I will, but..." Taggie shakes her head. "She's stubborn."

"I'll send some of my men to look after her. And we start immediately to show everyone you're mine, and under my protection. You'll need a dress for an event tonight."

I pull out my wallet and offer her the matte black credit card. The limit on it is enough to buy most houses three times over.

"Whatever you'd like, put on that. I'll arrange a car and security." For a second I consider dropping everything to go shopping with her. But that won't make sense if we've been married for a year. "Gavino and my core team will accompany you."

She's shaking her head.

"Yes." I lower my tone to one of uncompromising command. "A dress for tonight, and anything else you need. If you're going to be my wife—"

"Your fake wife," she reminds me, and that is unwelcome.

"You must ensure no one suspects. My wife knows she's valued above all. She can buy everything she wants, and I'll smile as I pay the bill."

A shadow passes over her eyes. "Yeah, but your *fake* wife—"

She stops mid-sentence when I reach out and place my fingers on her lips. "We won't repeat that again." My heart can't take it. "From now on, there's no fake. You're my wife, so that I can protect you. And we won't give anyone a chance to suspect anything."

She's warm and soft and unexpectedly yielding beneath my blunt fingers.

"Do you understand?"

The whites of her eyes show large as she looks up at me and nods.

"And you'll spend using my credit card as though it would be a personal affront to me if you didn't?"

Another nod, and a small part of me relaxes.

If the price of Taggie being my fake wife can be paid with that credit card, it'll be insanely cheap. I'd pay my entire soul.

6

TAGGIE

I always thought it would be great to be given a credit card, but it's terrifying. What if I buy the wrong thing? It's not my money, and somehow that's worse.

He's going to be cross with me.

The dress I bought is good, but is it good enough? I look down at the deep, shimmering blue of the full-length dress. I don't know what the fabric is exactly, but it's incredibly soft, and feels amazing against my skin.

It's wild that on Friday night I went to a club to get my first kiss, and on Saturday night I'm pretending to be married to the man who killed three people to protect me. Granny was sceptical about my staying with Dom, and I didn't even dare tell her about the fake wife thing. As predicted, she refused to come and stay here. Dismissed it with a "Pshh, don't be ridiculous".

"Taggie." Dom's voice comes from outside my door.

My tummy flutters. "Come in, it's unlocked."

"I thought I told you to lock your..." He stops mid grumble when he sees me, and stares in silence.

He's wearing a black tuxedo with a bow tie that's the

perfect amount of imperfect, and my mouth waters at the sight of him. My fake husband.

"Is it okay?" I ask nervously.

He sweeps his gaze down over my body.

"I know you said to spend lots, but it wasn't the most," I babble out with all the coherence of a three-year-old. "It was—"

"Was it the one you *wanted*?" he cuts me off.

I straighten. "Yes."

"Then it's perfect. You look perfect."

"Good enough for Richmond?"

"A credit to Richmond," he says sincerely, then adds with a wry twist of his lips. "Too good, really."

I can't help but laugh. "That's not true, you..."

I stop because I'm about to embarrass both of us. He looks delicious enough to eat without a spoon. I'd put my whole face on him and eat every part of him in greedy licks.

"I what?" There's a shadow over his expression, and something serious in his black-brown eyes.

"You look nice in that tux," I admit in a whisper. A spectacular understatement. He'd look amazing in anything, and I wish I could see him out of it, too.

"Nice," he repeats, with the inference that I mean it as an insult.

"Very nice." I'm blushing. I shouldn't be imagining him naked. He obviously doesn't think of me that way, whereas I'm hallucinating him in my bedroom at night.

Because it was a dream.

Wasn't it?

"Thank you, Taggie," he says roughly, and I go still with the sound of my name on his lips.

It's just because I'm a silly girl fantasising about a man out of my league when he's been kind enough to protect me by pretending to be my husband. It's not that he sounds like the man in my room last night... In my dream.

Is it?

All the way downstairs, Dom keeping a careful distance as though he's aware I'd climb him like a tree given half a chance, fancy dress or no, and I think about that dream. I've never had one like that before. The bit with the book was just weird, but the man I saw in the darkness was... Vivid.

Real?

"We're going to the Blackwood triplets' forty-first birthday and there will be a lot of the London Mafia Syndicate there," Dom explains when we're in the limo. "Hopefully there won't be any violence, except possibly from Mayfair if there are too many stupid jokes about maths. And all you really need to know about the maths club is that Rhys Cavendish wanted a baby with his now wife so badly that he pretended the mafia syndicate was a maths club so she wouldn't realise he was dangerous."

I snort at the idea anyone could marry a mafia boss without realising he was dangerous, then catch myself. Because I have first-hand experience of how deadly the man I'm pretending is my husband is, but I can suddenly understand why someone would make that mistake. Because there's an unshakable feeling in all my vital organs that Dom is trustworthy.

Dom tells me more about the London Mafia Syndicate as we travel to the event, filling me in on who's who, and that I should expect to be adopted by the wives and dragged along to their book club. No dragging needed, though.

Gotta admit, going straight from virgin who has never had a boyfriend to established wife cuts out all the parts of a relationship that I was most anxious about. I've never been interested in boys my own age, and only curious about older men in an abstract way, which is why I'm yet to have my first kiss.

When we arrive at the venue, worry spikes through my tummy.

Can I really carry this off?

Dom fits his arm casually around me as we walk to the entrance, his hand on the small of my back, and I stumble with the electric heat of his nearness.

"You're not scared of me, remember?" he murmurs, "And I'll protect you from anything."

"I'm not scared of *you*," I whisper back.

"You should be." He loses the words into my hair.

"Richmond!" A man approaches and stops dead when he sees me at Dom's elbow. "You have a plus one. Does that finally make you an addition to the London Maths Club instead of a minus?"

"Blackwood. Happy birthday," Dom grumbles with all the charm of a tiger woken from a much-needed nap. "May I introduce my wife, Taggie."

Dom keeps a possessive arm around me.

"Oh, not a plus one, a better half," says another man, with a slight Italian accent as he saunters up. He's identical to the first. They both have almost inhumanly bright-blue eyes and perfectly tailored suits, but when the first Blackwood triplet turns to his brother, a black tattoo is exposed at his collar, and the line of a gun under his suit jacket. These men aren't as tame as they seem.

"That is enough bad maths jokes," Dom drawls.

"It's not." The first Blackwood folds his arms. "Because finally, you solved the love equation, and you didn't invite us to the wedding."

I have to hide a giggle. They're ridiculous and fun, and

totally unexpected. Not what I thought mafia bosses would be like.

"Yeah, it was a lovely event." Dom squeezes me. "Just mia bambola and me."

"Mmm." The other Blackwood brother nods. "Looks as though they balance each other. He's an arsehole, and she's perfect."

"Well, that we can agree on." Dom smiles down at me, and I feel as special as they say.

"When is Sev going to get married?" grumbles the first brother.

"When he finds someone who's got his number." The second Blackwood brother claps Dom on the shoulder. "Come on, rompicoglioni, there are a lot of people you need to shock."

He's not wrong. It takes us a while to repeat our story, developing it a bit each time. Dom introduces me as *his wife*, sounding convincingly in love time after time. He describes dozens of romantic details that make my heart ache because I really wish they were true.

Roses. Phone calls. Sweet words and getting engaged after only a month. Our marriage on a beach in Sardinia. And although we met on a dating app, Dom says it was love at first sight.

All lies.

"Good girl," he murmurs, and I flush with warmth. "You're doing well. And don't worry, the London Maths Club isn't always this fancy," he adds as we move between groups, a pause in our introductions.

All around us are couples dressed in evening wear. As I watch, a man drops a kiss onto his partner's cheek, and a couple who have their backs to us, I notice the man's hand wander from her waist to squeeze her bottom. At the bar, another couple is kissing and laughing. No one seems to even notice.

"There are a lot of PDAs," I observe anxiously.

"Mmm. Come here, wife." He says that word with relish, but there's a soft tenderness in his expression, his dark eyes fathomless but warm as he draws me to him with the small touch on my chin. His other hand slides over my waist, until I'm flush with him.

He tilts my head up, and I boost onto my tiptoes to bring myself closer.

Brushing my lips with his thumb, he gazes down at me with naked desire.

Fake.

But although my brain knows that, my body doesn't. I tingle. I'm out of breath. My nipples are pebbled beneath this dress, and I'm hot and squirmy between my legs.

"How about a kiss so we're the same as all these other couples?" he murmurs as he dips his head.

"Okay," I breathe, and I get all the prizes for understatement.

Dom though, is an actor worthy of shiny gold awards that are heavy enough to brain someone with, because he lets out a groan like he's been longing for ten thousand years to kiss me, holding my waist and lifting me clean off the floor.

My eyelids flutter closed.

Then our lips touch, and I realise the disadvantage of faking that we're already married. Because my breath is stolen. He kisses me like it's his right to take my lips, my air, my soul sucked out through my mouth.

This kiss gives no consideration for the fact I'm inexperienced, or it's the first time we've done this. It takes. It demands and refuses to listen to anything but a moan of pleasure that inevitably is torn from my chest.

His tongue is in my mouth in a bold sweep, hot and possessive, as though I'm his fuck toy.

He shifts his hand and plunges it into my hair, careless of the hours the hairdresser spent making the curls beautiful, and I don't care either because he holds me gently but firmly, just pulling at my scalp enough to make me feel his strength and dominance over me. His power, all leashed for me.

My clit pulses.

This kiss is a whole-body experience, from my toes that are off the ground now as he presses me to him, to the tips of my hair, held in his big hand. Sparks shower through me as I feel a bulge in his trousers, hot and hard.

He's aroused. By me.

Then as quickly as he initiated the kiss, he sets me down and draws away. He meets my gaze and for a split second all my shock and confusion and desire are mirrored in his expression. Then his dark eyes glint with golden brown, and he smiles, soft and almost sad.

"You okay?" he asks.

"Yeah. Yeah. I..."

This is fake. That was a fake first kiss.

I flick my gaze to the side. One of the wives is watching us, while holding a baby, an indulgent look on her face as she talks to her husband. He glances over, then rolls his eyes.

"I think we fooled them. Not bad for a first go." I make light of it.

"What do you mean?" my fake husband demands.

"Just that I... Well." I'm blushing, and I wish I hadn't brought this up.

He waits, brows low, completely focused on me. It's as intense as his kiss, his attention. There's no getting away from it, but it's not like I want to.

"I've never kissed anyone before," I confess in a rush.

The shock that dawns on his face is almost comical.

"How..."

I think of my mother, having me far too young, and never seeing me grow up. I think of Granny's cutting wit, and emphasis that education and money are a better investment than boys who only leave you knocked up and penniless. I think of how none of the boys I know do anything for me.

And then I look into Dom's fathomless dark eyes, and I burn.

"Never had the right opportunity," I say.

He sighs, and reaching out, cups my jaw. "You should have told me," he rumbles. "We could have practised first so you weren't... Distressed."

"I wasn't." Quite the opposite. Although if you count horniness as distress, then yeah. I guess so.

How am I going to fake being Dom's wife when the way I want him is painfully real?

There's dancing, and it's a perfect excuse to not talk, and have Taggie close. Plus, stew in my own guilt.

I've always been morally grey, and never had my conscience bothered by decisions I made that were beneficial to me, but hurt others. When I've killed innocent people to torture Thaxted. When I've bankrupted people to make the deals that ensure Richmond as an area prospers and is beautiful, it doesn't disturb me.

Standing over Taggie's sleeping form and wanking off? Fine.

Lying to the men who are my friends in the London Mafia Syndicate by implying I had a hand in the murder of my whole family? Nessun problema.

But fuck, stealing my fake wife's first kiss?

Now I truly feel evil.

And I like it.

Because I do have a moral code—of sorts—and it's that I only take what's mine. Taggie's first kiss was mine, there's no question. But I'm forty-one years old. I took the first kiss of a girl who isn't yet twenty-one. I took the first kiss of a young woman in my care. I stole something precious and wonderful, and I think the reason I feel bad is that I would do it again in a heartbeat, despite knowing that this cannot end well. She's Thaxted's daughter.

What a joke that I imagined that faking she was my wife would be enough. I want *more*. The depth of feeling I have for the daughter of the one man I've ever truly hated, will sink me.

When I lead Taggie to the bar for glasses of water and she excuses herself to go to the toilet, my gaze follows her as she walks through the now-sparse partygoers.

I miss her already.

"Have you lost your watch, Richmond?" Feltham sidles up next to me.

I am known for turning up for a nominal amount of time to these meetings. Partly because in recent years there's an agonising number of couples and families, and also I still have residual guilt that it was a London Mafia Syndicate meeting that saved me from the same fate as my parents and siblings.

"Yes," I drawl. "I think I left it in the same shithole as you put your charisma."

"That's a very rude way to talk about my wife," he replies dryly.

I can't help but snort with laughter. "Only you Feltham. Most people name their dick 'Johnny' or something."

"The charisma is the stuff that stays in and gets her pregnant." He grins. "The deposition instrument is known as a cock. And if I find your watch where I like to put my cock, I'll kill you," he continues lightly. "And I suspect *your* wife would resurrect and kill you a second time, given how she's been glued to you all evening."

Chance would be a fine thing. She doesn't care about me. Just a good actress.

He catches the eye of the bartender and orders a Scotch and a glass of some fancy soft drink for his wife.

"How did you get anyone to be your wife, Richmond?" Feltham leans against the bar and regards me. "She saw past your familial homicidal tendencies, huh and agreed to marry you in secret because she was so embarrassed?"

"It's a Richmond family principle to only murder people who are dangerous and clever enough to be a threat, but I'd make an exception in your case," I add, and Feltham just laughs. Feltham is almost a neighbour of the Richmond mafia, and we're friends of a sort, having both been in the Mafia Syndicate since the initial meetings.

"And how come she's not pregnant yet? I don't think patricide is hereditary."

"Not everyone is as obsessed with having children as you are, Feltham." He's right that I am though. I'd love to make a new Richmond family with Taggie.

He grins unrepentantly. "Best thing I've ever done. My kids are great, and my wife is—"

"Thank you, I don't want to know." It was bad enough when I was just jealous of him in the abstract.

"Hey." Taggie touches my arm, and relief showers me as I see her.

"You'd like to go home and experience your husband's charisma, wouldn't you?" Feltham says to Taggie with an impressively straight face.

"Uh." She glances at me. "I suppose so?"

Shooting Feltham a dirty look, I take Taggie's hand. "Come on, that dance floor is calling to us."

While she comes willingly enough, and melts into my arms when we're among the few remaining couples dancing, moving with me naturally, I can see the questions in her eyes that I don't want to answer.

I'm reluctant to leave. That's the honest truth.

I don't like these events, usually. But I love faking with Taggie, and the moment we get home, it's all over.

8

TAGGIE

We're almost the last to leave the party, dancing until it was stupidly late, Dom's hands at my waist, spinning me around then back in for a kiss. I'm utterly seduced by this man playing my husband.

But the second we're alone, he carefully puts distance between us, and the teasing tone disappears from his voice. He stops flirting with me, and touching me, and instead asks simple questions about whether I've enjoyed myself and which of the other wives I like best. I hardly know the answer to the last part, since I spent nearly all evening with him.

He walks me upstairs to my bedroom door, and pauses. "You remember there's a lock."

It's not quite a question, or a command.

"Yeah." It's on the tip of my tongue to ask if he came to my room last night, but I swallow it down.

"Good night, Taggie."

Then he's gone. No kiss goodnight. No sign of affection.

I really, really thought he liked me. When he kissed me earlier it was the most magical, special moment of my life. I was stupid enough to think that maybe what he said about falling in love at first sight was a little bit true. I thought he found me attractive and interesting.

But it was just a show.

I stare around at the beautiful room, with all the things I wanted, and feel hollow. They're lovely, but unlike spending time with Dom and him touching my waist, and murmuring that I'm his good girl, they don't make me feel warm and happy.

I feel so stupid.

I'm not tired, merely sad. Pathetic and unloved. I could stay up and read, but I don't. There's no way I can fall asleep, though. Apart from anything else, I don't want to wake up again from a dream that Dom is in my room, unable to tell the difference between what I long for and the bleak reality that he's not attracted to me.

Why would he be?

All the evidence I gave myself for Dom's interest seems flimsy now I've discovered how easily he can turn off that loving-husband act.

And yeah, I thought I'd seen him before, but he's not the only tall, dark-haired man with tattoos and black suits in London. I must have been mistaken, just like I was dreaming last night.

I crawl under the bed covers, cold and alone.

I don't sleep, thoughts circling. The covers are around my shoulders, high and snuggled in, protective against the chill of Dom not wanting me.

It's the sound of the door handle that I hear first. Then nothing.

"Taggie." My name is an almost silent breath. "Mia bambola..." There's a cascade of low words in Italian that I can barely take in, never mind understand.

I can't believe it. That's my fake husband's voice.

Remaining motionless, I listen intently. There are soft sounds of fabric shifting, but I can't identify them, and my heart is beating so loudly I can't think.

Could I risk...?

I open my eye closest to the pillow a tiny sliver.

And yes.

My heart bursts.

It's Dom. Here. In my bedroom.

He's standing next to my bed, looking over me. He's bare to the waist, and his chest is covered with tattoos, the black ink snaking over his body. It makes him even more beautiful, and a bit scary.

"What is it about you, bambola? You're such a good girl, but you make me a bad, bad man. I crave you. See how hard you make me?"

He rubs over the huge bulge in his trousers, and yes, I do see.

"I've done a lot of evil things, Taggie. I'm not a good person. I've killed many, many people."

That statement rockets electricity down my spine in an unexpected way. Am I excited that he's a murderer?

"But I don't take advantage of innocent girls under my protection..." He groans. "I've never wanted to have a girl so much that I even considered something so sick as to..." He trails off. "Fuck, you're so perfect, and so young. It's wrong for me to be doing this, but the alternative..."

There's the sound of a metal zipper, and I dare to peek my eyes open to see as he pushes down his black underwear and reveals his cock.

I bite back a gasp. Even fuzzy from the darkness and my mostly-closed eyes, my eyelashes obscuring him, he's huge. The head is red and angry, and veins pop out, snaking down the length. There's no way I could get my hand around it. It's beautiful, and intimidating.

I totally get the big deal now.

"At least if I'm doing this while you're sleeping, I'm not touching you when you're awake. I'm not telling you how I can't live without you."

He strokes his fingers roughly over the swollen tip, and huffs out a breath.

"Cute kisses in public, and I wank my obsession off in the dark." His voice is barely above a whisper. He's not talking to me. He's talking to himself. "Do I just need to get this out of my system?"

He grips his cock hard with that black-tattooed hand of his, and makes a gruff noise like a wounded animal.

Between my legs is getting hot and squirmy as he strokes himself with firm, rhythmic movements. My mouth is watering, and I don't even know why. Do I want to eat him? My jaw suddenly longs to open and have that massive length pushed inside.

"I need you so much, Taggie." His voice is low and intense. "I've never wanted anyone like this. It's a hunger I can't sate. I need you."

Heat flares through me, sparkling at my core. As subtly as I can, I press my thighs together under the covers, and yes, yes. It shoots a thread of pleasure into me, but not enough.

The intensity of being the object of his desire is heady. I might only be the girl he watches while he pleasures himself, but the sounds he's making, and his words, tell me this is not a casual thing for him.

"I want to finish deep inside you. I want to spray right up into your womb."

Ohh... I didn't know. But yes. I'd love to be filled up with Dom in every way.

"I can't have you in truth, Taggie. You're too young and innocent. I'd be corrupting you. Dragging you into a sordid mafia world you don't deserve."

His hand is moving fast now, and the tip of his cock is getting bigger, and redder.

"My good girl. I'd get you pregnant if I could. Make sure everyone knew I'd fucked you and made you *mine*." He groans, and it takes all my strength to lie still.

There's no way I'm interrupting this.

I know the moment he comes. The rounded, blunt, end of his cock swells further and in the split second before he puts his hand over it, I see white liquid shoot out.

The shock of it is intense, and I'm as wrecked as he is.

I'm also, as I lie there, observing him clean up and pull his trousers over that huge cock, undeniably aroused.

Watching Dom wank while hearing him talk about me was the single hottest thing I've ever seen.

I feel special, and seen.

Even when he leaves, with a gentle, "Buonanotte, bambola," I remain awake, my skin feeling a size too small. The impulse to roll over and put my hands between my legs to feel what I know will be a flood is almost unbearable.

One thing is for sure. That was not a dream.

9

DOM

The restaurant opening in Richmond means I've had all evening with Taggie, and I tell myself that our romantic dinner, with plenty of opportunities for small touches to her shoulder, and kisses to her hair, has sated me. She told me about the books she'd read from the library in her room, and her eyes sparkled when she tasted the cheesecake for dessert.

I try to bury myself in work, firing off emails requesting updates from the men guarding her grandmother, and reading the report from the cuckoo. I'm gratified that the death of Thaxted's sons has hit him hard. He's angry.

Keeping Taggie safe, and torturing Thaxted, I shouldn't need more. But she compels me like no woman ever has.

I mean to go to bed, but my feet take me where I crave to be, despite my mind yelling that I mustn't. I hold my breath as I try her door, and the relief when it's open is almost enough to make me fall to my knees.

Then when I see my fake wife, I go weak all over again. I was already hard in anticipation, but seeing her like this, blood rushes to my cook. I'm solid. Throbbing.

She's wearing a small, strappy top, and the covers only reach to her waist. I can see far more of her breasts than a man twice her age ought to. Her face is upturned, and the moonlight highlights one side of her serene features. She smiles slightly in her sleep.

"You're so beautiful." My whisper is a little raspy.

I don't want to wake her, but I need to be with her, so I approach and stand over her bed. With a reverent fingertip, I trace the line of her cheekbone over to her ear, and down her neck. Unlike me, she's unmarked. No scars. And she's soft, so incredibly soft.

"I should stop." But I don't.

It's pointless to resist. I keep trailing down to the gentle wing of her collarbone, then further.

"Your breasts are perfect little handfuls, bambola. They'd look so pretty with my come on them."

I groan as I feel the curve of her breast, nudging aside her top and yes, just as I thought. She is made for me. My hand fits over like we were designed together, rather than the reality that we were born decades apart.

Her nipple pebbles beneath my palm, and it's too easy to imagine that she's awake and welcoming my touch. Out of the corner of my eye I see a movement, or I think I do. But when I flick my gaze from her breasts to her face, her eyes are closed.

She's not awake. She would say something if she was. She'd run.

Continuing my exploration of the exposed parts of her with one hand, I free my cock with the other and begin to jerk it, slow but rough.

It's dry, and it would feel better with lubricant. But the sharpness of it as I stroke is right.

"You make me so hard. I don't deserve you. I wish I did,

but... fuck. I can't leave you. If all I ever have is these moments, and your joy at books and dresses, could that be enough?"

It's a question. I don't have the answer.

"My hunger is growing," I admit as I accelerate my hand movements, the tendons in my forearm bulging.

And it's not even her breasts that I have stopped my fingertips on. No. I recognise through my arousal that it's her soft throat, where her pulse beats fast for a sleeping creature.

"Are you dreaming of me? Dreaming of your stalker who loves and adores you?"

I've never said that to any woman before Taggie.

I mean it.

"Ti amo così tanto. I'm obsessed with you."

I look up to her closed eyes and moan as my orgasm barrels through me and out of my cock.

Just in time, I withdraw my hand from Taggie and place it over the blunt head of my lock, catching it in spurt after spurt.

The pleasure tingles down my spine. Good, but not satisfying. Not really, when what I most want is her hand. Her mouth. Her wet pussy and her dark-blue eyes on me as I make it bliss for her and me together, so she screams for more.

"You're mine, Taggie." She doesn't respond. Of course she doesn't. She's asleep.

"I want us to be a family, and you to wear my name for real. Not because you're scared, but because you love me."

It's a raw confession.

"I need to be inside you in every way."

I sigh as I look at her. I can't have that. Can I?

A glance down at my hand, and to her parted lips and a filthy idea occurs to me.

So wrong. And yet even as I tell myself that, I'm sitting on the edge of her bed—good thing this is an outrageously expensive mattress, so it only gives beneath me—and bending over her.

I scoop white ejaculate onto my fingertip, and hold it just above her mouth, watching with savage delight as it drips in.

"That's it. Take your husband's come. Swallow it," I murmur.

She doesn't. But it calms some primal part of me that I'm inside her. My seed is on her tongue.

I need more.

Wiping my hand carelessly on my underwear, I shift so I'm braced fully over her, one fist on either side of her shoulders.

"It's difficult to explain this feeling, Taggie." I don't know why I'm talking to her as though she can hear. My girl obviously sleeps like the dead. "I want to be *part of* you."

I brush kisses over her cheeks, soft as rose petals, then pause.

"My sweet little doll." Pursing my lips, I let a drop of saliva fall, stretching out until it connects us, until finally it breaks and it's there.

Another small bit of me, in her.

I wish it were a baby. One day, I swear, it will be my baby filling her belly.

10

TAGGIE

"Is there a way to make my bedroom hotter?" I ask as he walks me upstairs at the end of another night of socialising. This was a less formal event, a dinner party. Dom sat next to me, his arm around my shoulders, as I chatted with Jessa Lambeth about fairy smut. He didn't talk much, just listening and toying with my hair. Dropping the occasional kiss to my cheek with measured affection.

Always the distant gentleman, my fake husband.

I'm going to try to *break* him.

Dom shoots me a dark look. "You're cold?"

"A little." I wonder how far I can take this? "I think I'd sleep better if it was warmer, and I wasn't squashed under the blankets."

"You're finding it difficult to sleep?"

"Oh, no, I reassure him. I just wake up cold." And alone. "I thought it would be nicer to be warm. Granny's house is always warm. Probably too hot for most people." I laugh and cross my fingers behind my back to dispel the lie. Surely Granny wouldn't mind me slighting her excellent housekeeping if she knew it was such a good cause.

A horny cause, admittedly.

However perfectly he plays the loving husband in public, he never touches me when we're alone and I'm awake. But last night's brushes of his hands on my skin have kindled a burning need in me. I want him to lose control.

So I'm going to lure him. Tempt him. If he needs me to be asleep to reveal his desires?

Okay. Game on.

"I'm used to sleeping without any covers." Absolute untruth. Is my nose growing? "So can I turn up the heating?"

It might be, judging by how Dom is looking at me.

"Yes," he grits out. "There's a thermostat. It's—"

"Will you show me?" I want to get him in my room, like I'm a nineties pop song.

He nods with the sort of reluctance usually reserved for major operations and situations where someone could die.

"I looked around here for it." I gesture at the bookshelves containing the special editions. I've been thinking about these a lot, especially since Dom added to the collection at the charity auction. "But I could only find these amazing books. I couldn't believe you have this author in particular." I tap the spines of the hockey romances that I was reading only last week. "I love them, and they're indie published so not in the usual bookshops."

My fake husband looks more uncomfortable than a penguin in a sauna, and swallows. "Mmm."

"I wondered how you ended up with them?" I ask innocently.

"The thermostat is here." He turns away, and moves to behind the door, where there's a little panel.

Well. Of course it is. I knew that.

"Ooo, thank you." I follow and deliberately slide in close.

He sucks in a breath as my arm brushes his. We do this in public all the time, but now we're alone it has taken on a frisson of the forbidden.

"There..." He hesitates as I get closer under the pretence of looking at the temperature. "I've turned it up for you."

"Maybe a bit more?" I suggest, leaning across him, seemingly to reach the dial.

He jumps back as the side of my breast touches his chest. Even through the layers of his formal clothes and my dress, contact between us is electric, as though in the short minutes since we were in public with a reason to be all performative affection, it's built up a static charge.

I need more of him, and I have to know what the truth is here. My devoted husband when we're on show, the carefully distanced man when we're alone, or the gritty guilty, obsessed lover I saw last night.

"I'll leave you to it. The room should warm up quickly, so hopefully you'll sleep well."

"I'm sure I will." I'm looking forward to tonight.

He gives me a jerky nod, and strides to the door, then hesitates.

"You can lock this," he reminds me.

"I know," I say lightly. "But it's safe, isn't it?"

"You're always protected in my house," he replies roughly. "But I'd rather you *felt* secure, so you should lock your door."

"I feel good." When he touches me, I feel wanted and cherished. I had no idea there was so much power in being desired.

There's something about the way that Dom said he

needed me last that makes my spine tingle. Safe, yes. Because no one hurts someone they need.

I smile innocently.

He scowls.

"I'll try to remember."

"Good night, bambola," he growls, and swings the door shut behind him.

"Good night!" I chirp back, then add under my breath, "For now."

11

DOM

Hotter.

My god, as though she isn't hot enough.

When I walk to Taggie's room that night, I'm certain the door will be locked. But no. She insists on torturing me.

As I open the door, a wall of sub-tropical heat meets me. How does her grandmother pay for her bills? Does none of her family know about sweaters? Are they secretly desert lizards?

I strip off my shirt as I approach, because it's so fucking hot I'm nearly sweating. And that's before I see her.

My perfect doll. She's laid out on top of the covers of her bed, on her back, one arm over her stomach and the other at her side. And she's almost naked. Her breasts are revealed, small and perfectly formed. Little ski-slopes topped by berry-pink nipples.

I was already hard from anticipation, but fuck. Seeing her like this... Her legs are slightly open. Tantalising. Her smooth thighs and shapely calves are bare. And there is a triangle of plain white cotton over her sex.

It taunts me.

That simple pair of knickers say, clearly, that she is not for me. She's young, and inexperienced, and not the sort of woman meant for a forty-one-year-old mafia boss with grey in his hair and crow's feet around his eyes if he ever smiled. Which I don't.

But even knowing that, I'm drawn to her like she's a siren. I can't help it.

"Taggie," I breathe. "Did you do this for me?"

She sighs in her sleep, and I let myself believe it's her saying, yes.

"You're unimaginably beautiful like this, bambola." I should keep quiet if I can't stay away, but it's impossible. "Your body is made to be pleasured. I want to touch you and make you feel good more than I want..." I think of the revenge I've built my life around for the last two years. My sole aim before I met this woman. It all pales. "Anything."

There's space on the side of the bed for me to sit, and I stare at it, pain in my chest. Of course, my cock is aching, desperate to be jerked off harshly. Or to sink into soft, wet, heated flesh... But my heart hurts too. I need her so much, and she'll never want me in return.

"Taggie, are you awake?" I say, a little louder.

Fuck knows what I'll do if she stirs. Make up some bull-shit about the fire alarm going off because she turned the heating up to the temperature of the molten sun, I guess.

But she doesn't. She continues to breathe deeply and evenly.

I shuck off my trousers and let them fall to the floor, then ease myself down onto the space it feels like she left for me. An invitation like the unlocked door.

The things a man will do to justify his obsession.

I'm not deluding myself. I know I'm a filthy bastard.

"Don't wake up, bambola," I whisper and ghost my

fingertips down the outside of her thigh. Her skin is like silk. "I'm too old and dangerous for you."

This is going to escalate. I knew it would, but I have this crazy feeling in my chest unlike anything I've ever felt before. It was an egg cracking open inside of me, birthing a dark monster when I first saw her. And since then it has grown, feeding off every time I've seen her. And now...

The monster is in full control.

I skim my hand up her front, pausing at her breasts, then further, to lightly rest over her neck where her jugular beats. Faster than I'd have expected for a sleeping girl. She's such a tiny thing. Like a mouse in my palm, all rapid pulse and soft, breakable, fragile little body.

"It's okay," I mouth as I shift down and ease her thighs apart. "I'm going to take such care of... Ohhhh."

She's wet.

Her knickers are soaked through. That's the first thing I see as her legs fall open.

"Such a good girl." I can't believe it. "Is all this for me?" It's not, of course it's not. But the fantasy is too delicious. I bring my fingertip to the cotton. It's warm and wet.

I ease the fabric to the side, revealing her pink folds in dark shadow.

My touch is gentle as I slide my fingers over the seam of her sex.

"You're so delicious, bambola. That means doll in Italian," I tell her, playing with the fantasy she can hear me and is as turned on by this as I am. "And right now, you're so like that, aren't you? My little doll."

She's overflowing, like she was getting herself off moments ago, rather than asleep. Perhaps she's having very sweet dreams. Filthy dreams of her protector and his rampant cock.

"Forgive me. Forgive me, bambola." I'm hoarse as I plead for her to excuse what I can't stop myself from doing.

I slide one finger into her folds, and immediately, she yields. Soaking me, sucking me in.

"You're like touching the sunrise," I still, in awe, even though my heart races and my cock twitches. I nudge further into her wet cunt, and there it is. That small, hard nub that is the centre of her pleasure. It's so easy to glide over it, and she pulses as I do it again.

Then again.

This is a step too far. Absolutely depraved.

"I've always been able to control myself before. But with you. You're... You're different, Taggie. I feel..."

Fuck, can I say this?

She's asleep. She'll never know.

"I feel so connected to you." I rub in gentle but slowly increasing in intensity circles over her clit. "You're the piece of my life I've been missing all this time. I know it's not really like that. I know that's a lie I'm telling myself to excuse the inexcusable. But it's true that I've never done this before. I've never wanted to. I've never even thought of it. You're so young. You're not meant for me..." My voice breaks on that last word.

The pain of acknowledging how intensely I feel about this girl, while simultaneously knowing this can never be what I most need, is almost unbearable.

She writhes in her sleep, and I'm so far gone, I don't stop. I need her to come, even if she's asleep. Even if she might wake.

"These stolen moments, bambola. You can't know what this means to me, even though it's wrong. It feels..." I take one long breath, then another. My finger is soaked up to the second knuckle now.

With firm movements, I stroke her over and over, stimulating her body. I hold my breath, waiting for her to break. Reaching for my cock, I rub the pooled pre-come over the shaft and fist myself. I barely need anything. I'm impossibly worked-up from touching Taggie. It's only seconds, and I push us over the edge at almost the same time, her core pulsing around my fingers as I spurt over my belly.

I groan.

It's stunning and yet, without her eyes on me, it's hollow.

I clean up, and set her thighs together, then stand over my sleeping girl.

"I can't shake this stupid thought that you were made for me," I murmur. "Or perhaps, I was made with space inside my heart for you, and all these years it's been waiting, being empty. I've been lonely without you, Taggie. And now I've seen you, and it's clear how perfectly we'd fit together, the pain of not being with you has flared up. It's revealed like a light revealing a gaping hole I've been ignoring."

12

DOM

It's a measure of how desperate I am for public events to bring Taggie to that I find this acceptable.

"A blind book charity auction?" she asks as we enter the hotel that's hosting this evening's excuse to have my hand on the small of my wife's back, I mean important fundraising and philanthropic opportunity.

"I don't understand either," I reply.

We're here at one minute past the time on the invitation, because I am as patient to have Taggie in public so I can touch her as a hungry tiger is for his tea.

"Taggie!" Lily Anderson greets my fake-wife as though they're best buddies and I reluctantly allow her to be pulled away for a hug.

We're supposed to have been married in secret for a year, I remind myself. This level of obsession is going to get suspicious. But like the threat from Thaxted and the inevitable choice of how to deal with him, I'm pushing the risk to the back of my mind and relishing the present.

"I don't know if I said," Lily is telling Taggie. "I'm the

owner of a bookshop in Croydon, and Willow has one in Bethnal Green."

"So what's a blind book auction?" Taggie glances around at me. "Dom couldn't tell me."

Lily raises her eyebrows and tuts. "Not book boyfriend material."

"Her book *husband*," I growl, and draw Taggie back to me.

The noise in my head and the thudding of my heart immediately quiets. She's a drug, and I'm willingly addicted. Taggie sinks into my side, wrapping an arm around me, and my inner monster calms.

"Too right," Lily agrees with a grin to Taggie. "The idea is a cross between a charity auction and a blind date with a book. Various donors—some requiring more persuasion than others—have agreed to give books from their collection for free to be auctioned in aid of our chosen charities. And the twist is, they describe the book, but you don't see exactly what it is until you've bought it. Surprise!"

"Oh my god that's awesome!" Taggie squeals.

Lily hands us both a program. "Don't miss Lambeth's book."

"Wouldn't dream of it," I say dryly.

The event turns out to be a whole dinner and after dinner thing, and it takes us a moment to find our table.

I drape my arm over the back of Taggie's chair and listen indulgently as she reads the auction list from cover to cover. The listings are all the most influential of the London Mafia Syndicate, and Taggie shows what a perfect mafia wife she will be—would be—by effortlessly recalling all their names and territories as well as details about the wives she's met. Around us, the room fills up.

We're joined by Mayfair, Lambeth, and one of the

Blackwood triplets, and their wives. No children, but there are some on other tables. I don't look that way, not just because I'd rather watch Taggie, but because it gives me an ache in my chest that, while it's been present since my family died, it's definitely worse since I met Taggie.

Champagne cocktails are served as an aperitif and Taggie takes a glass with adorable excitement. Her eyes sparkle, as she tries it and finds it sweet and bubbly and decadent. But when Blackwood's wife selects the sparkling flowery soft drink instead, Taggie notices immediately.

"I'm pregnant," explains Ella Blackwood with a rueful laugh. "Inevitable really."

People congratulate her, and joke about babies, and when Taggie glances up at me, my stomach swoops. Her expression reflects the longing I've tried to repress: to have a family to love and care for.

I have a flash that she can see my hidden desires. It's like she sees past every barrier I have. Then she looks away, blushing, and I know it was an illusion.

Yes, she's the only one who knows about my revenge plot, and how it hurt me to lose my parents and siblings. Not even the members of the London Mafia Syndicate, who helped me when Richmond became my responsibility, know that. But she thinks I'm helping her out of kindness, and she believes she can leave anytime.

"Anyway, enough baby talk. Who's bidding on the signed special edition of Blythe's?" says Ella.

"Not bidding, but I was curious," Taggie replies. "Who do you think the author is?"

Then they're off, trying alternately to get out of the book donors what the book is, speculating from the description, and wondering how much they'll go for.

As we eat dinner, I listen. Taggie is passionate about

books with sprayed edges, whatever that means. It turns out there's more to this evening than my stated aim of showing off our relationship and my covert aim of touching Taggie when she's conscious and pretending that she loves me. Because winning auctions for my wife is totally within my skill set.

When dinner is over, Lily and Willow introduce the auction, and Westminster takes the stage and talks about how important these charities are. I play with Taggie's hand as Westminster drones on that although London's taxes pay for lots of the needs of London's most vulnerable, and each mafia does its part, there remain people who slip through the gaps.

"Is he really lecturing mafia bosses on taxation?" The kingpin of Rotherhithe leans over from the neighbouring table and asks in a stage whisper, his Russian lilt stronger in his irritation.

"Do you pay any taxes?" Lambeth replies in the same tone.

"No." Well. I do. A bit.

"I think there was a tax I paid once," Rotherhithe says thoughtfully.

"No, that was a taxidermist," Mayfair says deadpan. "Terrifying, that stuffed wolf. The Bratva kids seem to have taken it as their mascot and pretend to ride it."

I glance at Taggie, and her lips twitch with mirth, though she's looking straight ahead and seemingly listening to Westminster, who is still talking.

Lambeth nods. "Easily confused."

"Yes, you are," Rotherhithe grumbles, but smirks. "Who's afraid of the big Bratva wolf, Mayfair."

"Enough of that," one of the women from the audience yells. "Time for books, Westminster."

There's a collective intake of breath as Westminster's hand twitches as though going for a gun. But he instead pulls out a credit card, and grins. "My beautiful wife is correct, as ever. Gentlemen, we'll be needing these..."

A ripple of relieved laughter goes through the room as he saunters back to Anwyn and sweeps her up for a kiss.

Jealousy stabs at me, and I have to look away. I wonder what it would be like to have that. A genuine relationship. A marriage based on trust so deep that it can stand a public... whatever that was.

Lily and Willow invite Blythe Blackstone onto the stage for the first auction lot, holding a brown-wrapped oblong that is large enough to do some damage in a fight.

"This is a spicy fantasy romance, signed by the author, in an *exclusive* leather-bound edition..." she explains.

Taggie's face is a picture of longing. She's gripping my fingers and her eyes are glistening.

I don't understand buying books. Never have. But I do understand wanting something beautiful and special. I totally get the desire to possess that's so strong you'd do unspeakable things to have it. After all, for two years, that has been revenge, and my life. And after a week, that obsession has been eclipsed by Taggie.

The bidding starts and Taggie's shock as it increases is such a delight.

I let my colleagues have their fun, battling over it. There are gasps around us at the price reached when Canary Wharf finally bails, and Taggie has covered her mouth, eyes wide.

"That's so much!" she whispers to me.

"All done?" Lily says as the rival bidder folds.

My hand shoots up. "More." I wasn't even noting the

amount, I was watching the only thing that matters to me: Taggie.

"What?" Lily looks at me like I'm crazy.

"Just more," I clarify. "Whatever he bids." I nod towards Streatham. "More than that."

"Richmond has finally lost his marbles," says Lambeth idly.

"Ten thousand more?" asks Streatham, glancing at his wife. "What do you think, Sophia?"

"Ten more on top," I counter immediately.

Taggie grasps my arm. "What are you doing?"

"A hundred." Streatham's tone is irritated.

"Sure," I reply, then add to Taggie, "Getting you the book you want."

"Hundred and fifty?" Streatham offers.

"Let him have it since it's important to the newlywed," Sophia says before I can also up my bid, and shoots Taggie an indulgent look.

My fake wife just blinks back, not understanding.

"Fine," grumbles Streatham. I'm on my feet in a second, and there's applause as I weave quickly through the tables to the stage, and take the wrapped book from Blythe.

"Enjoy," she says, and winks at me.

When I return to our table, everyone is smiling except for Taggie, who looks faintly alarmed. Then as I sit and place the book before her, her expression shifts to all-out shock.

"Dom, I..."

"Open it," I tell her roughly. "It's a late wedding present, bambola."

Someone coos.

"I can't!" she says in panic, glancing around. "It was so

expensive." But she has picked up the package, and turns it over in her hands.

"It's for *you*."

"This is insane," she murmurs.

"No." I reach out and touch her cheek, regarding her with all the real affection I feel on full display. "This is love."

Her breath hitches, and her lips fall open.

I smile as I take the opportunity and kiss her lightly on that pink bow of a mouth.

There's new brightness in her eyes when I draw back, pretending that such moments are commonplace for us, and that they don't affect me intensely.

Every moment is fresh with Taggie. Each kiss is more meaningful.

She brings a finger to her lips and brushes it, giving a little laugh. "Your beard is scratchy."

I smirk. "You love it."

And the shyly pleased expression that she gets then makes my blood sing. She's mine. She doesn't realise it yet, but she's mine forever.

"Open your present, bambola," I prompt.

This time she obeys, carefully peeling off the ribbon and the tape and then pausing to relish the pulling back of the brown paper... to reveal a book. Leather-bound, chunky.

She lets out a squeal of excitement and runs her finger over the raised gold lettering on the cover.

"I knew it!" Lina crows.

"That is gorgeous!" Jessa peeks over from the other side of the table.

"The jealousy around here right now," laughs Willow from the stage. "We should start the next auction lot so Richmond can have his thank-you kiss."

Taggie blushes the cutest shade of pink and I grin. Hell yes, I'll have a thank you. Maybe even take one tonight...

I swore I wouldn't go to her room again, but as she cautiously puts the book down as the description for the next book begins, I know that's a lie. I cannot stay away from her.

"Thank you." She gives me a peck on the cheek.

Nice. Cute.

"Fuck it," I growl, and pull her onto my lap. "That's not enough."

I take her lips greedily. She's across my thighs, and her body is so slight and tiny—the doll that I call her—and my cock responds automatically. She's everything. I kiss her with every bit of possessive feeling in me, and what's baffling and wonderful is that she kisses me back.

Taggie lets out a little whimper and curls her fingers into my lapel, and I hold the back of her head and her waist, like if I let her go, she might fly away from me.

"I love you." I don't realise I've said it aloud, right into her mouth, until she says too and my heart takes flight.

I press my forehead to hers, my eyes closed.

Fuck. If this is faking, and reality is that Taggie doesn't love me and won't whisper those precious words, then I'll stick with the charade. Reality can go fuck itself.

Over-fucking-rated.

We miss the entirety of the next auction lot, but by the time the third begins, I have Taggie comfortable on my lap, but thankfully not touching my hard-on, and have managed to stop mauling her.

She sneaks looks at her new special edition fantasy romance, one finger tracing over the dragons on the cover. But her hand remains on my chest, over my heart.

I wonder if she can feel it beating for her.

On stage, Felicity Brent is describing a book as old, and an OG romance, whatever that means.

"Oh..." Taggie presses her lips together.

"What is it?" I toy with Taggie's curls.

"I think I know what it is! The book, that is," she explains.

I nod. "Would you like it?"

"Felicity says it's a first edition of the book that first got her into reading historical romance, and has a scene where they think two side characters have scandalously run off to Gretna Green in Scotland to be married."

"I see." But I don't. Obviously, I don't.

"I think it's a first edition of Pride and Prejudice!" Her eyes sparkle and the excitement buzzes out of her. "How amazing is that!"

"Very," I reply seriously.

She continues listening as Felicity finishes up, and the bidding begins.

I know what I'm going to do this time. What my love wants, she gets.

It costs me the amount of money people usually spend on a house to have that book—it turns out to be a set of three books—handed to Taggie when she jogs up to the stage in that gorgeous dress. But when she sits back down on my lap without checking with me, as though this is just how we do things and we're the kind of in love that means I'm her chair whenever she needs and I can kiss her neck as she unwraps the books I won and bought for her, I have never been happier.

I feel like a lion bringing an antelope to his lioness.

Her glee when she finds her guess was correct is better than any lucrative deal I've done. The way she reverently flicks the pages makes my heart light.

I love her with everything in me, so spending money on her feels right.

The following book is a copy of Lina's debut, and Taggie is so excited to find that her new friend is a romance author that I buy that for her too.

"This book is responsible for the best blow job I've ever had." Lambeth's voice cuts through our curiosity about Lina's book with his announcement of the next lot.

"Really?" someone calls.

"I said what I said." Lambeth grins unrepentantly and winks at his wife, Jessa.

"Moisture damage isn't acceptable in books you're giving away," Westminster says wryly.

"Did he stick his cock in it?" shouts a voice from the back of the room.

Lambeth laughs good-naturedly. "Okay, correction. This book *inspired* the best blow job I've ever had."

Taggie giggles and blushes, catching my eye.

There's fierce bidding, mainly from the mafia wives, but also from a few of the men.

"You're not going to bid?" she says as Willow announces the end of the auction, and I stay silent.

I raise my eyebrows. "That would be for my pleasure."

She looks even more confused.

"Little bambola." I stroke her cheek. "I am all about your satisfaction. Every day, in every way."

The next book is an exclusive advance copy of a fantasy series, that isn't even a proper book but rather printed pages because it isn't published yet. Taggie listens with interest, but I don't get the impression she's as desperate as many of the other book-girl wives, who are exchanging passionate theories when they hear it's the long-awaited finale to books that have been adapted for television.

"Do you want this one?" I ask softly, as the pitch ends.

"No." She shakes her head. "I didn't like the ending of the television series. I'm not convinced the books will be better."

"Let's start the bidding..." Lily trails off as Mortlake strides onto the stage and holds out his hand for the book.

"Sir." Lily stands straight and looks him in the eyes. Croydon's wife is braver than she appears. "You have to wait until the auction has finished."

Mortlake doesn't reply, just nodding, and leaving his palm up, as though still expecting the book.

"Do you want to bid?"

Another nod.

"Anyone else?" Lily asks, voice higher than usual.

"A hundred thousand," Westminster calls.

Mortlake stares at him.

A single nod.

"Two hundred." This from King's Cross.

"Three."

"Four."

Mortlake glowers.

There's total silence as he nods after every amount, until Lily shoves the book at him and says, "I think a million will do."

He returns to his seat, and instead of opening his prize as everyone else has, he sets it on the table and crosses his arms.

It's a good thing Taggie didn't want that one.

"Will we never know what it was, do you think?" she whispers to me.

"No." Mortlake is frankly disturbing, even for a Bratva.

But we win the next auction for the hockey romcom Taggie wants, and an advance review copy.

As the rest of the evening progresses, she unwraps book after book, with joy and disbelief, and I think, *over and over, if I'd known you sooner, bambola, these would have been your birthday presents. Christmas presents. Every good thing that you missed from not having a father, I will give you now.*

Seeing her unwrap special books, and know she's special, fills my heart, because this isn't fake. She is the sweet, unknowing antidote to everything bleak and dark in my life, and somehow I need to keep her with me.

13

TAGGIE

"Can you hold on a second while I fetch a glass of water?" I ask as we walk back into the house, Dom carrying my pile of books. I pull the small pack of tablets from my clutch.

"What are you taking, bambola?" Dom snaps, but follows me to the kitchen, and sets down my presents with a scowl. When I casually hold out the packet, he snatches it up and glowers down at the poor cardboard. I'm surprised it doesn't combust. "Where did you get those?"

"Just some sleeping tablets," I say innocently. "I got them from Jessa Lambeth."

"Why?" he growls.

"To help me be out for the count." *So that you'll do more to me.*

I think Dom would have stayed out until dawn, buying me books and being all couply, and I don't understand why. He's so deliberate about being attentive to me when we're in public. And I think we both want more closeness in private too, but the moment we're alone it's like there's a force field around me.

Except when he thinks I'm asleep.

And I've been thinking about his name for me. Bambola. My fake-husband calls me his *doll*, and all evening as he spoiled me with extravagant books, I pondered how to repay him.

And that was when it occurred to me. If a doll-wife is what he wants, then that's what I will be for him. I can goad him into giving in to what we both desire by being exactly the doll he calls me.

"Have you not been sleeping well?" There's worry around his eyes. He doesn't return the packet, turning it over in his big, black-inked hands.

Hands I want on me. Unrestrained.

"Oh no, I've been sleeping fine." The sleep isn't really the issue. It's what he won't do to me before I sleep.

I need more.

"Then why drugs? It's not good to—"

"I'm just so wired after the book auction. I don't think that coffee was really decaf. I'm going to put the books on the shelves, but afterwards, I don't want to lie awake for hours, you know?"

He looks disturbed as he returns the tablets to me.

"Thanks." I smile up at him and toss the pill into my mouth. His brows draw together as I bring the glass to my lips and use my tongue to push the pill to the side just before I take a sip of water, tucking it into my cheek. His gaze dips to my throat as I swallow.

He's not breathing, and I hide a smirk.

I lie on my tummy, because maybe he'll find it easier if he can't see my face. I leave on my knickers at first, but then, I think about it, and wriggle them off, leaving them on the bed next to me because Dom said he liked them. But the logistics of getting them down my thighs or out of the way? Nope. I want him to have complete access.

It's a long wait, and I can't relax. I'm vibrating with need, my nipples hard on the covers.

Eleven comes and goes.

Last night he didn't delay so much, and I'm convinced he will be here before midnight.

The grandfather clock in the hall chimes twelve and my mood slumps.

Perhaps he won't visit?

I convince myself of it. Maybe he doesn't want me, and isn't interested in using my body as he said he was. Does it disgust him that I took—pretended to take—sleeping tablets?

It's a long time after twelve, but before one, when the door handle twists.

There's a deep, masculine sigh.

"You should lock your door when you're out-for-the-count, bambola," he whispers, his voice hoarse and tortured. "Are you awake?" he adds a little louder.

Keeping my breathing even, I remain totally still.

"No, you're asleep, bambola, ready to be defiled by a man who loves and needs you so much he can't help himself. I can't keep away."

The wash of relief as I hear his steps across the carpet towards my bed is almost as good as an orgasm. He's here. He's come for me.

I feel the moment he sees me fully. I left on a light in the corner of the room, and I know it highlights my bare body. My bottom sticking up. My hair over my shoulders. My face is in shadow, but one of my knees is raised.

And it stops him dead, exactly as I'd hoped.

"Fuck..." He sucks in a breath. "You're naked. If you knew what it does to me, you'd run."

Right into his arms, yes.

"You would definitely lock your door." He groans. "You're the most perfect thing I've ever seen, and you can't be mine."

I love the way his Italian accent comes to the fore when he's aroused. It's sexy as all get out.

Focusing on keeping my breathing calm, I ready myself and hope. I hope so much, though I'm not sure exactly for what. For him to touch me, yes. But I need him to go further than he did last night.

His fingertips on my shoulder are unexpectedly tender and soft, then he sweeps an unmistakably possessive hand down my body, over my hip.

"You're so beautiful, bambola," he says, almost reverently. "Exposed, and mine. I can't wait to do this when you're awake... I want to see your eyes looking up at me." He sighs. "But that's not going to happen."

He skims his fingertips down the dip of my spine, and when I guess a man who was restraining himself would stop at the base of my back, he doesn't. A deep, wounded sound comes from his chest as he trails a path between my buttocks and to my bared slit.

"Have you been thinking of your monster, coming to get you tonight, bambola? Did your dreams make you a horny little toy for me?" It's a rumbling tease, and it makes my clit twitch.

His fingers find my clit and stroke right over it in a move so confident it's pure arrogance. It's taking, even as it's giving me pleasure. I wish I could rub my aching nipples against the sheets, and push onto his hand, begging for his cock.

The touch to my bottom is rough. A possessive grasp. Now he thinks I'm unconscious, all his base desires have risen to the surface. Then his hand is gone and there's just the rhythmic, insistent strokes to my clit.

A chink of metal, the whoosh of leather. A button pops and then the sound of his zipper is the perfect harsh music. The shh of fabric being pushed aside.

I strain to hear him stroking his cock.

I can't at first. The wet sounds of his fingers on my pussy and the spiralling feeling of pleasure obscure it.

It's his groan that reveals that he's touching himself slower than I was expecting. Like he's rubbing his cock up and down with the intention to enjoy it, not just get off as quickly as possible.

"You're unbelievably lovely," he whispers. "My good girl. I don't deserve your perfection."

This is better than anything I've ever felt. He somehow knows my body, pushing me further and further into pleasure with his fingers. I'm close, just needing a small bit more. A missing part. Then there's a touch at my entrance, and pressure.

His finger slides into me, satisfying in the moment and yet not enough a second later. I pulse, and he moves faster.

"You're so wet, and my god. Such a needy little pussy. Grasping at my fingers. My good girl needs something bigger don't you?"

Yes. Yes, I do. I've seen his cock. It's magnificent. Scarily big, but I want it anyway.

He continues to pump into me, rubbing his thumb over my clit. I've touched myself, sure, but it has never felt as all-encompassing as this. He senses my body like we're tuned to each other.

I'm writhing, right on the brink, crazed with the intensity of my desire for *him*. Dom.

"I can't." He sounds like he's trying to convince himself of something. "I shouldn't." He groans. "But my god. You need it, don't you?"

I do. I really do.

"A toy... But there weren't any on your wish lists or social media posts, were there? So I didn't buy you one."

What? What has that got to do with it? The question slips away. I don't care as much as I crave my fake husband.

"All I have to satisfy you is... I shouldn't."

You can, I tell him silently. Do it. Please.

"You trust me, and you're sleeping."

There's the rustle of his knees as he shifts closer.

"But your sweet, weeping, needy cunt..." He groans. "Just the tip. Just because a pussy this soaking wet needs a cock to hold."

Something hot and blunt and silky brushes my inner thigh and I bite the inside of my lip to keep my face impassive, and not cry out. Then his frighteningly large bulbous end touches where I'm slick.

I can't help the sound that emits from my throat.

"It's okay, bambola," he soothes me. "It's almost a pacifier. This will make that empty little cunt of yours feel better."

He pushes against me, achingly slow, until there's a pinch. But it feels right, and my clit throbs.

He lets out a stream of Italian words I don't understand. I can't even tell whether they're praise or a prayer or swear words. Maybe they're all three.

"Bambola, you're so tight."

I'm close to coming. Inside, I'm screaming, desperate. I keep my eyes closed, a whine tears from my throat.

More. I need something more. Just...

Then like a cork popping into a bottle, there's a complete change between us. An extra fraction of an inch into me, and the fullness hits a pleasure centre I've never felt before, and I'm coming, the white light of it rolling over me from where we're joined.

Vaguely, I hear the now-familiar raw sound of Dom orgasming too. Inside me. Even through the spasms of my ecstasy, I can feel the wet heat he's filling me with, and the way it overflows.

Then there's just our breathing and the silence as the pleasure ebbs away, leaving contentment.

I really want to open my eyes and see what he looks like. What is he thinking? But I don't have to look, because he tells me.

Dom strokes the hair from my cheek and kisses me tenderly. "I love you so much."

I love you too. I say the words in my head. They feel right.

I've fallen in love with the mafia boss who cherishes me when we're pretending to be a couple, and when he thinks I'm asleep, but won't admit to any emotion when it's the two of us alone.

I've broken through this barrier he put between us of him being too old, and the special bond we share being only fake.

He came inside me. The power of his desire has given me a secret: I could get pregnant.

"That was..." He gives a rueful laugh. "You coming on the tip of my cock? That was the single best thing that's ever happened to me, mia bambola. And knowing I spilt my seed in you is a close second. A precious gift. Thank you."

He continues to place soft kisses over my cheek and neck, until we're both breathing evenly again, and I'm so relaxed and happy, I might actually fall asleep.

My fake husband doesn't feel so fake now.

"I need to clean you up." The withdrawal makes me instantly empty and I long for that closeness. His steps go to the bathroom, and a tap runs. Then he's back.

"We made a mess," he says teasingly, then hums with pleasure as his fingers move over my pussy.

"Fuck, bambola." He exhales roughly. "My sleeping beauty. There's blood."

He breathes out, hard.

And I get it.

It's perfect. Whatever happens, I will have the sweet memory of how I lost my virginity to a wonderful man I adore. A forbidden man who I love. And who I know now for sure, loves me.

He continues to use the washcloth to clean my sopping pussy lips.

"I don't regret it though..." He slides one finger into my passage, and I have to bite down on my lip to keep from moaning. "Push a bit of seed further up."

Kissing the dip in my lower back, he slowly pulls his finger out, and his weight shifts away from me.

"Buonanotte. Sleep as sweetly as you deserve."

Then there's the soft noises as he withdraws and lets himself out of my bedroom.

I lie exactly where he's left me, motionless, for a long time. Despite his attention with the washcloth, I'm slick between the legs, and I think about how he put his sperm further up into me. As though he'd like it if I were pregnant.

I could be *pregnant* with Dom's child.

That spreads a warmth through me. The most delicious secret. I know that he might have made me pregnant, and he doesn't know that I know.

14

DOM

The theatre is full. It's a charity concert, and I'm scraping the barrel for public events to take Taggie to, because this is fucking *opera*.

At least the private box—a little closed-in area with just two seats, high at the side of the theatre, looking down on the stage—gives us space and the illusion of privacy.

Taggie looks amazing in a floor-length light-blue dress in a silky material. It's strapless and reveals her creamy shoulders, and when I saw it, I very nearly vetoed leaving the house.

Except, then I wouldn't get to touch her.

The show starts, and there's immediately squawking in Italian. I pretend to listen, but all my attention is on my fake wife.

"What's it about?" Taggie asks me in a whisper, after a few minutes. She has given up on the little binoculars provided.

"I think it's going to be a tragic love story," I mutter back, leaning close. I breathe in the scent of her, and all the singing is suddenly much more bearable. We watch, tilted into each other, arms brushing.

I needed this. Taggie next to me.

"Do you want children?"

My head snaps around.

Taggie is looking up at me questioningly, with her big eyes. That sweet pink bow of a mouth is wet, and my heart is trying to launch out of my body through any location it can. My throat. My ribcage. My stomach.

How does she know?

"Children?" I gasp.

"Yeah. I believe it's something married couples do," she replies teasingly, keeping her voice low, even as the music soars.

"Why do you ask?" I'm in a panic. Feverish almost. I'm hot and cold, and I think there is sweat trickling down my spine.

She doesn't know. She can't. The idea that women have magical powers that allow them to recognise they're pregnant is absurd.

It isn't possible. She was *asleep*.

"I was just thinking about how we could be even more convincing as a couple," she replies. "And I've always wanted to have a baby."

Oh fuuuuck. Why did she have to tell me that?

"I wonder if we should pretend I'm pregnant," she muses quietly, turning her attention back to the stage. "Maybe the Essex Cartel won't believe you care about me if I'm not pregnant."

"What?" No one could possibly think that, because it's not true. Taggie is the centre of my universe.

"Kids are permanent, right?" she adds. "Without kids,

or if you don't want kids, Thaxted will assume I'm disposable. Just a first wife."

"No." The idea of faking that is too much when she might be pregnant for real.

"But you said Richmond is all about family—" she begins.

"It was until the rumour I betrayed and had them all killed." I press my lips together and stare at the stage like it did me personal injury. I see nothing.

The two of us starting a new family would heal parts of me I hadn't fully realised were broken. I want this far too much.

"Would you like to have children with me?" she continues, "Would you mind if I got pregnant?"

I flick my despairing gaze at her. I deserve this torture. No question. But my god, I had no idea she'd emotionally waterboard me. Especially after last night when she was mia bambola, pliable and innocent.

When she could be pregnant with my child, right now, and *not know*.

"I'd get a big belly." She places one hand on her flat stomach, and giggles softly.

Inwardly, I groan. The image is instantly in my mind, of Taggie full of our child. My cock thickens.

"That wouldn't put you off, would it?" Her hand creeps onto my thigh.

I make a strangled noise.

"What was that?"

"I…" I cannot lie to her. "It wouldn't put me off you," I grit out.

"Oh good. Because I don't have much experience. Well. Any. I'm a virgin."

My teeth clench. *No, you're not.*

She casts her gaze down and although one hand is on my knee, the other is behind her back. My brain is so far into overload with this conversation and her touching me in a way nobody could possibly see—so it's not strictly part of our pretending—that I can't understand the significance.

"And so many of the other wives in the London Maths Club—yes, I call it that now, sorry—have children. But I wouldn't want us to even pretend you've got me pregnant if that grossed you out."

"It doesn't," I reply faintly.

"Oh good. That's a relief. You know," she gives a little chuckle. "Just in case I pretend. Or if I were pregnant... One day."

Okay, this is cruel. Below us on the stage, the woman is singing a big, mournful song about how her love is unrequited, and yeah.

I get it, universe. Seriously? More subtlety, please.

But I don't regret anything I did last night though. I can't.

I look at Taggie again.

She blinks back innocently. For a second I'm so sure that she knows everything that happened last night, and she's doing this on purpose...

I thrust away the idea.

Absurd.

That is not how a young woman responds when she finds out that a man twice her age is so obsessed with her that he let himself step over a line when she trusted him with an unlocked door, sub-tropical bedroom temperatures, and a sleeping tablet.

I should be strong enough to withstand the temptation of her. I've never had this issue before, but then, Taggie is on a different level. I cannot control my desire for her.

And suddenly, I know what I have to do.

Scare her.

My sweet bambola is playing with fire, and I need her to realise that. She must find out the danger she's in.

"But I'd like to be clear," she insists. "Would you want me to be pregnant?"

"Taggie." I take her hand from my knee, and drag us both to our feet, her chair falling over with a noisy thud I'm sure draws attention.

Never mind. I only see Taggie.

In a second, I have her pinned against the side of the box. There's a curtain only slightly obscuring us from the rest of the audience, and nothing to block the view from the stage if the performers were to glance up.

"Is this what you wanted?" I bite out, lowering my head so my lips are close enough to ghost a breath on her lips. I can't kiss her. There's no to see, and that isn't our deal. "For everyone here to assume I'm so horny for my wife that it pains me to last two hours without having her?"

She pants.

"Perhaps you want them to think I'm obsessed with getting you pregnant, and would do anything, even fuck you in full public view, to ensure my seed takes at exactly the right moment?"

A little whimper tells me I'm on the correct path. But even if it didn't, I'm not sure I could hold myself back from saying this.

"They already know you're *mine*, Taggie. Everyone thinks we bang like rabbits because you're so irresistible. All the people in this theatre suspect you'll be swollen and fertile with my child in the months to come. That I fuck you as hard as you deserve, and make you scream."

I draw back enough to look into her blue eyes. She trembles. Her arms are pinned above her head, and she arches into me.

This girl is so innocently seductive. My cock throbs with the need to take her. Fuck her and claim her as mine in truth.

"Now, are you going to behave?" I ask, with dangerous softness. "Or do I have to make you?"

The excitement in my chest as she casually swallows a sleeping pill when we get back that evening is wrong, so wrong.

But I can't deny it. I'm instantly hard.

The rest of the evening at the opera with Taggie was as torturous as the day without her. I might never focus on anything, ever again, that isn't her.

She might be pregnant.

This is a house of cards, for sure. One breath, one shaking hand, and it will fall. Taggie will try to run, I'll stop her, and she'll hate me for keeping her captive.

Or she'll figure out she's carrying my child—she will sooner or later because I don't think I can stop having her—and the tentative friendship we've built will collapse.

"I'm bushed," she says, and covers her mouth as she yawns.

Why does she need the tablet if she's tired?

"I'm off to bed." Standing, she approaches with a sweet smile, sliding her little fingers into my lapel. In a trance, I lean down. I grunt a reply as she gives me a chaste kiss on the cheek.

It burns.

"Goodnight!" There's something in her eye, a glint, as she casts one last look over her shoulder.

I don't tell her to lock her door. I couldn't bear it if she locked me out tonight.

I *need* her.

For the first hour I sit with my head in my hands, alternately telling myself this is the last time, or I won't go to her ever again, and knowing I can't prevent myself tonight or any other night going forward. All I can do is pray she doesn't wake.

Then I go to my office, and attempt to work. I reply to the messages from the cuckoo—Harrison—about Thaxted. Apparently he's discovered that I killed his three stupid sons. There could be consequences, and I ensure my men are informed of the heightened threat. I increase the security at the house, and allocate two more to guard Taggie's grandmother.

Then I go through numbers and reports, making myself look at them.

I swear four hours pass, but it turns out to be twelve minutes when I check my watch.

Then after an agony, I shower. My cock is stiff and thick, and I stroke it as the scalding water beats down on my head and runs over my chest.

I don't make myself come. I save it for her.

I'm a perverted fuck, but I'm going to do it again. It doesn't hurt her, I rationalise as I pad silently down the corridor to her room. I haven't even bothered getting dressed. I'm not pretending this time. My hair is still wet, and I'm naked, my rigid cock beading with pre-come. It's past one in the morning.

She took a pill, and she left her door unlocked when I told her repeatedly not to. Taggie is in my house, and she belongs to me and that she doesn't realise is a small inconvenience.

I hold my breath as I swing open the door, then my head spins.

Her naked body is entirely exposed, and she's asleep on her back, bathed in the light from a small lamp.

"My sleeping beauty. Mia bambola." I slip into Italian, praising her in a low, hoarse tone as I approach and stand over her peacefully resting body that I'm going to defile.

I run my fingertips over her creamy white thighs, and over her soft belly. Her legs are parted, as though in welcome. It's her way of sleeping, but my brain interprets it as an invitation that her right leg is bent and angled upwards, revealing the pretty pink petals of her sex.

And they're wet.

There's no hesitation tonight, just hunger.

Eagerly, I get my shoulders between her knees, and my face where she smells like she's mine. I take one, long greedy lick.

"Delicious."

She quakes beneath me. I put my mouth on her and suck. I devour her. Gorge. Cover my cheeks with her cream until her hips are chasing my tongue and my cock is hard and aching.

"I can't wait, bambola." It's a rough admission as I lever myself up. "Forgive me." I crawl over her. "I know you need to come, but I have to feel you. It'll be just the tip. Only for a second. You'll never know... Until you're perfectly rounded with our baby."

I run my hand over her belly, imagining I can feel a curve.

"After hearing you say you wanted children..." I've given in to all my most feral desires. "Fuck, I can't wait to see you pregnant." And pray she forgives me.

Delicately, I lean down and kiss her mouth.

Her breathing isn't quite even. It's shallow and fast, and something at the back of my head shouts *no*. It roars that I should stop.

But my lust is too strong. I can't listen to logic.

"I love you," I whisper as I reach down and notch us together, then pause, choked. Because it feels so right. She's incredibly silky and yielding. Made for me.

And yet she isn't. She's asleep.

I tell myself it's for the best.

"You feel like heaven," I murmur brokenly as I push into her past the resistance of her body that's there even though she's soaking wet.

"Taggie, you're so beautiful." I sweep my gaze over her luscious little tits. The sight of the tip of my cock wedged into her soaking pink folds almost causes me to lose control. But I grit my teeth. Because this time, she doesn't clench around me, tipping me over.

That's a good thing. Surely. I'm not disappointed, because I get to be inside her and kiss her.

I want to be deeper, to have her, to spill right up against her womb and make her pregnant. But this will have to be enough. A sweet dream.

I drag my gaze up, shaking at the sight of her. She's breathing a little fast. I'm going to steal another kiss while I make myself come in her entrance. Just the tip.

Reaching to my cock, I pump the exposed part of the

shaft then sigh as I lift my head to kiss her lips, as though she wants this.

The shock is lightning.

Because a pair of midnight-blue eyes look up at me.

She's *awake*.

16

TAGGIE

We stare into each other's eyes for long seconds, neither of us moving. The tip of his cock is wedged into me, and my greedy, wet pussy is grasping at him.

I want him to take me properly. To make me his and know I belong to him. No more faking being married and keeping a careful distance between us the rest of the time. No more pretending to be asleep and biting my lip to keep from moaning because it's so good and I need him so much. And while I enjoy the tease, I'm desperate for him to lose control.

"Dom." My voice is shaky.

I bring my hands up to touch his face, and quick as a snake, he has one wrist pinned above my head, then the other too, my arms stretched out, his bent.

He shifts so he has both my hands held with one of his, and I gasp at how vulnerable I am. There was a power in seducing him with just my body, but now his almost-black eyes are boring into mine and I'm helpless, a bolt of fear goes through me, sharp and vivid.

"I'm sorry." He swallows, then closes his eyes. Every

line I can see of him is taut. His jaw is set, the muscles in his shoulders tensed, and his hips haven't moved, keeping precisely the same pressure on my needy pussy, not withdrawing or proceeding.

"Dom, I—"

"Tell me no," he interrupts harshly, eyes flying open again, tortured. "Say no, right now, and I'll leave, Taggie. I'll find another way to protect you from Thaxted. I swear. I can't take back what's done, but—"

"More."

He doesn't respond, his expression awestruck. Like he can't believe his ears.

I wriggle my hips, trying to get him deeper inside me.

"Taggie." He sounds strangled. "I can't resist... Fuck."

"Then do it." I lift my knees until I can wrap my legs around his waist, and he groans as the action slides him an inch further.

"Taggie," he breathes, and this time it's amazement and joy. He cups my jaw, sliding his fingers into my hair. "Do you want this?"

"Yes." I nod as a rainbow of expressions flicker over his face. But it settles back on concern.

"This isn't a casual thing for me, bambola." He huffs, as though this is costing him effort, and slides his free hand through my curls to cup my neck. "If we continue, I'm going to keep you. You'll be mine, forever. I'll love and protect and be territorial of you. My wife for real. And fuck, I'll breed you with so many babies. All the kids you were talking about, and more. I'll love you until I die and then beyond into whatever void or afterlife there is, because *nothing* will stop me loving you." He pauses, brows tugging together, and I long to smooth them. "I love you."

"I love you too," I whisper and as his expression of shock

and disbelief changes into pure happiness, his dark eyes soft, my heart responds by melting.

"I don't deserve you, but if you love me..." His grip on the back of my head tightens, and he groans. "I'll take it."

Then he's sinking into me, slowly, oh so slowly stretching me open, and it hurts because he's huge, and it's everything I've ever wanted because he's breaking me and remaking me to be his. He stroked himself harshly when he thought I was asleep, but he's strong but gentle with me now.

"That's it," he murmurs. "Breathe through the pain. You're being such a good girl for me, taking my big cock so well."

Then his mouth lands on mine and he's kissing me, deep and intense, his tongue invading my mouth pushes his cock into me. His naked, hairy chest is pressed onto my breasts, my pert nipples sensitised and sparking with every small movement. Flickers of pleasure as the pain eases into fullness.

"You're heaven. So tight and hot and wet," he rasps against my lips. "Say it again."

"You're mine, Dominic Richmond." And that's not what he meant, but his groan tells me he needed to hear it.

"Mine. I was going crazy without you. I can't breathe without you."

He bottoms out, our hips touching, his balls resting on my bottom. They're big, and even as I focus on opening for him, allowing the pinch to ease into pleasure, I think of all the seed they hold, and how he's going to fuck it into me.

I tug my hands. He lifts his head, and his fingers tighten on my wrists, those dark eyes glinting as he considers my implied request. For a second I think he's going to keep me held.

Then he releases me, and this is trust, I realise. He was worried I wouldn't want him. This gorgeous, powerful, gentle giant thought he was too old and too brutal for me.

Cupping his face, I tilt my hips so he goes deeper and thread my fingers into his short hair.

"I love you. Make me yours in every way."

He stares into my eyes and makes a sound like a wounded animal, then begins to withdraw, just an inch. It's uncomfortable, but the slide back in tears a whine of pure pleasure from my throat. "Yes."

"Taggie. Please," he says brokenly as he eases in and out of me again, then again, faster, and all the discomfort fades away into bliss.

"Yes." I tug his head down until his mouth touches mine, and he's all the way over me and inside me. He's overwhelming. His arms are braced on either side of my head, stroking my hair, tugging a curl just hard enough to stimulate every part of my scalp and down to my toes.

"I'm never letting you go," he murmurs around our kiss. He's fucking me properly now, in long thrusts that send tingles through me.

This act is possessive in a way I didn't anticipate. He owns me, using my body as surely as he did when I was pretending to be asleep.

"You feel so tight and hot. Such a good girl for me. You were made to be mine, to take my cock."

The sensation blooms between my legs, building, and it makes me weak. I focus on it, allowing my eyelids to drift closed.

"Look at me," he demands, and I reopen my eyes. My handsome fake husband is glowering down into my face. Intimidating, powerful, scarred, and *darkly beautiful*. "You keep your eyes on me. No pretending that you don't want this."

He's savage, and so close to me I've never felt anything like it. We're connected as closely as two people can be.

Then he cracks a sliver of space between us, and crams his hand into it. I don't understand for a second, then his blunt, strong fingers touch my clit, and a cry emerges from my throat.

"I want you to come on my cock, and watch me while you do." He swipes firmly across my clit, and it bounces from his attention, sending streaks of pleasure through me. "See that it's me making you feel this way."

He speeds up, smiling evilly as I whimper. He's so deep inside me, he's touching parts I didn't realise could be felt.

"Come for me. Give it to me."

I can't look away. Arrogant, demanding, but I love this man with every part of myself he awakened and all the places that had been so alone until he found me.

"Come for me, and I'll give you a baby."

"Dom, Dom," I sob his name as the wave of my orgasm crests over me, even stronger with his whole length pistoning in and out than anything I've felt before.

"That was..."

"What was that, bambola?" He sounds affectionate and amused, and I'm a puddle of girl. I'm warmed jelly.

"Better than any time you've made me come before," I confess.

He stills, and the soft, indulgent look is wiped from his face. "You were awake for that?"

Oh... I didn't think this through.

"Meep!" I don't even know what that word was supposed to be.

"You were awake?" His voice is thunder. "And you didn't let on?"

17

DOM

In an instant, everything changes. That's why I wanted her like this.

We were made for each other, so of course she'd bring out savage desires that lay dormant for all these years. Because she has them too.

"You little minx," I growl, and shove myself deeper into her, making her gasp. "You were teasing me."

She looks up at me and a smile blooms on her face, going from caught out to a grin so naughty it needs a health warning.

"Well, now you're in for it." I pull out with a wet pop. Her expression switches instantly to indigent and disappointed, I can't help but laugh as I flip her over onto her stomach, then grab her hips and drag her onto all fours. Then I've rammed my cock back into her, hard.

She cries out at the sudden intrusion. Whatever else you can say, I've been delicate with her. But fuck, she lured me in?

I'm taking what's mine.

"Such a perfect brat," I tell her. "You're." Thrust.

"Going." Thrust. "To." Thrust. "Take." Thrust. "This."
Thrust. "Cock. Whenever I need you to."

Keeping one hand tight on her thigh, I grab a fistful of
her impossibly soft blonde curls and tug. She whimpers and
angles herself so I go deeper, hitting her cervix with every
punch of my hips to hers.

"Dom. Please."

"Please what?" I demand.

"What?" I'm not gentle now and my voice is so deep
and harsh, I barely recognise it.

"Use me," she whispers.

Then I lose control, going wild. Pumping into her,
chasing my orgasm as she arches her back and moans,
tipping her head to one side then the other. Getting her hair
pulled harder, I realise, and oblige, and that makes her moan
beautifully.

"You'll be my doll, Taggie," I pant. "Mine to play with,
fuck, fill up. Put a baby in here." I reach around and push
my palm into her belly. And through her soft, yielding
tummy I can feel my own length driving into her, rear-
ranging her insides with each thrust.

Fuck, but I like feeling how I'm invading her, making
her mine.

My balls tighten.

"Going to breed you, my little wife. My teasing,
naughty girl. I love you so fucking much. Mia bambola."

"I love you too." Her fingers dig into the bedcovers and
her head tips back. "Make me yours. Make me pregnant.
I..." She runs out of words as I slide my hand between her
thighs and ruthlessly circle her soaking-wet clit. "Please.
Please, Dom."

"Si. Si." Then I'm pounding her as I hold her hips up
with one hand and rub her in time with my thrusts. I babble

in hoarse Italian, telling her again how I love her, how she's my world, how she's going to pay for teasing me on her knees and on her back and with her pussy over my mouth and my cock in the back of her throat. I tell her how we're going to have so many children, filling this enormous house with our family and making it ring with laughter and joy.

I keep on fucking her, holding on by a thread as pleasure threatens to overwhelm me. I can't even speak now. Emotions crowd my chest and block my throat as ecstasy spirals at the base of my cock and tugs at my balls.

But there's no need for words. Love is enough.

She cries out and collapses as another orgasm hits her. The way she clenches around my cock is too much this time.

White-hot waves crash from her body into mine. I jet into her, giving one more thrust into her tight heat. As I come right up against her womb, and through the blur, I imagine that seed going deeper still. Exactly where it's needed to put a baby in her.

It's blasts of pleasure that wrack every drop of my blood as I spurt into her, but it's love too. Sheer relief, and so much love that I'm literally bursting with it. I can't speak. My mouth is open in a roar that turns into a grunt and my expression must be feral, but Taggie is looking at me over her shoulder like I'm a god.

Her face is full of the same love and wonder that is pouring out of me. I keep my eyes open, and so does she, openly watching me, our gazes connected. And I think it's that which makes it the longest and most intense orgasm of my life.

She ruins me.

As I fall onto my hands over her naked body, totally destroyed, there's a sheen of sweat on both of us.

It's all I can do to roll to the side and bring her with me, holding her close to my chest, my cock still inside her.

"I never dared to dream..." I murmur when my heart rate has dropped sufficiently that my mouth works for anything more than kissing her head and neck.

I feel more than hear her laughter. "But you gave me dreams, didn't you?"

18

DOM

This peace. I've never felt anything like it.

I wake with the feeling I'm twenty and able to bounce between clouds. And the first thing I see? Taggie. Still asleep, lashes fanned on her rosy cheeks.

A smile tugs at my mouth as I remember that we barely slept. We talked. We kissed. And we had filthy sex where I bounced her on my cock, pounded her into the mattress, and took her from behind as I told her over and over that she's my good girl.

I sweep a wayward curl of hair from her face, and her eyes flutter open and fix on me.

There's a split second where I think I've dreamed this whole night and I'm about to see her horror, but then she wriggles closer. Her breasts touch my chest, and her hands link around the back of my neck. I groan, even as I can't take my eyes off her, and my cock—which was already hard with morning wood—goes to rock.

"Good morning, husband," she murmurs, and hell, she's so sultry, this girl will be the death of me.

I yank her flush to me, growling softly with appreciation as my cock is pressed between our stomachs.

"Taggie, I need to feel you again." My hand is at her thigh, lifting it to my waist and opening her.

"I'm yours."

Shifting her upwards, a rumbling growl comes from my throat as the tip of my cock finds her wet slit.

I reach between us, and grasp my cock. There's a flash of confusion in her eyes as I don't go to thrust into her.

"I imagine you're sore," I explain as I ease over her folds.

"I'm not!" She writhes against me, and I feel her crossed fingers on my skin.

"Mmhum. But we've established you're a liar." I squeeze her waist and continue rubbing her as though my straining, aching cock is her sex toy.

Then I get to the right spot, and there's no complaints from her. I make myself crazy with the feel of her hot wet slit, just out of reach, but I won't hurt her. Not now, not ever.

Though when her eyelids droop closed, I kiss her cheeks and growl, "Look at your husband as he makes you come, Taggie."

"Sorry," she gasps, and does as she's told.

"Good girl."

The praise sets off another flurry of spasms that I feel at the end of my cock, and it's absurd how every moment is better and better with Taggie.

"I don't think I'll let you close your eyes as you orgasm ever again, bambola," I tell her as her orgasm ebbs away.

"Dom." She tries to pull me into her, but it's like a leaf trying to shift the sky.

Luckily for her, I'm inclined to do as she wants.

"Just the tip." I grin as I nudge her folds apart and stroke my cock—covered with her cream now—once, twice, three times, until I topple off the same edge she did, coming in her entrance.

When we've kissed and recovered, I carry her into the bathroom for a long shower. I wash her carefully, as though she really is the doll I call her, and she traces the lines of my tattoos with her fingertips.

"Do you want to wait until you've finished your degree before we have our wedding?" I ask as I dry her off with an enormous fluffy white towel. "Or shall we—"

"You want to get married for real?" She stares at me.

"More than anything in the world. It might need to be a 'renewal' of our vows though."

She throws herself into my arms and I lift and hold her tightly, my chest expanding with happiness. Nothing could spoil how perfect this is with her.

"Breakfast and wedding plans?" I suggest after long minutes of cuddling that we both needed. Craved.

"Granny will be so excited!" she exclaims. "I'm going to call her!" She grabs up her phone, but her face falls the next instant.

"What is it?" But I know. Of course I know.

Taggie passes me the phone, trembling, her eyes filling with tears. "This is all my fault. I should have convinced her to stay here."

Granny:

I've got your precious Granny.

Tell Richmond he has one hour to bring you to me to swap, or she dies.

. . .

Taggie begins to weep, and I gather her into my arms.

"We have to save her," she sobs. Or I think that's what she says.

"We will, don't worry." I'm thinking, ideas spidering out in my mind. This isn't exactly the scenario for Thaxted I had planned, but I can make it work.

I have to.

That makes her cry all the harder. "I don't want..."

"Shh, shh."

Taggie:

I'll be there. Richmond.

Immediately there's a message in return with a location and protocol for unarming. Standard sort of stuff.

"I can't go to him." Taggie's face crumples. "But I can't leave Granny with him either."

"You won't have to, and she'll be safe with us, back in Richmond, this afternoon. Together. A family." I'm already figuring out the scenario and details as I pull her into my arms, comforting her.

"But how are you so certain?" she whispers against my chest.

"Because I've been planning revenge against Thaxted for a long time, bambola."

"He'll know you're coming, and he'll know you're angry." She swallows and looks away, her pretty face full of pain.

I take her chin between my finger and thumb and force her to tilt her head until she's looking me in the eyes.

They're Thaxted's eyes. I hope we ensure she never

feels bad about that, because while I'd happily cut those same eyes out of her father's head, on Taggie, they're the most beautiful thing I've ever seen.

Even when they're surrounded by pink and full of tears.

"You won't have the revenge you wanted, and I'll..." she trails off sadly.

"Thaxted won't be as tortured as I was losing all my family. But perhaps he never would, however long I tried. A man like that won't ever love anyone the way I love my family. The way I love you. We'll get your grandmother back, and you'll stay with me."

"Maybe." She still looks worried. "It seems awfully risky."

"It's not." I would never put Taggie in any danger. "I have something he doesn't expect."

She blinks. "What's that?"

"A cuckoo."

19

TAGGIE

Dom told me not to be alarmed when I saw my grandmother tied up—or worse—but it's still a shock that she's on the dirty warehouse floor on her knees. She's wearing the neat, tailored trousers that are her trademark, with a turtleneck and pearls. And she has a black eye. Her reading glasses that hang around her neck are cracked.

But she's bright eyed. Defiant.

I'm shaking as we approach the middle of the cavernous space.

"It's alright," Dom murmurs, his arm over my shoulder.

I trust him. I do. Dom told me the plan, yet I'm still nervous. What this man's sons nearly did is fresh in my mind.

"Agatha." Thaxted's smile makes my skin crawl. "Welcome." He's a tall, skinny, blond man like his sons, with blue eyes and an oval face. He's wearing a pink shirt with a pale blue sweater, tan trousers, and brown deck shoes, as though he's going boating, not torturing my grandmother.

I don't reply.

Dom's grip on my shoulder tightens. "Let Mrs Hayes go."

Thaxted barks a mean laugh. "Give me the girl first."

"Don't do this, either of you," Granny says, gaze darting between Dom and me.

"I'm not leaving you." My voice is steady, which I'm proud of.

"Taggie has my name, you know. We're married," Dom says to Thaxted. "And the Thaxted name will fade into obscurity."

Thaxted's face goes ugly with fury. "I won't have my family polluted—"

Dom grins. "Too late. The curse is happening, isn't it?"

"Your stupid bitch of a mother got what she deserved," Thaxted spits, and glances at the younger man, also blond and blue-eyed, beside him. The cuckoo, I realise. Harrison.

"Taggie," Granny says clearly. "I want you and your man to leave. Now. He killed your mother too."

What? She knows what happened to my mother?

A cunning look crosses Thaxted's face. "Richmond has been stalking you, Agatha. Aren't you curious to know why?"

That's not a denial, and though I never knew my mother, a burn of anger streaks through me.

"End this," Granny insists. "Leave. Please." Her eyes implore me.

I crowd closer to Dom. "And I don't care."

That stops Thaxted, but only for a second. "Aw," he makes a fake sound of sympathy. "You haven't told her why you *actually* want her, huh, Richmond?"

I feel Dom go stiff beneath my fingers.

"Harrison here will tell you that I usually wait until my children are twenty-one before I inform them about their superior heritage." Thaxted gives Harrison a proud glance. "I made an exception for you and sent three of my sons to fetch you early, since you're the last of my children."

For a second I can't process what he means.

"I'm your father, Agatha," Thaxted says, low but confident.

The statement reverberates through me like an earthquake. I stagger, and Dom goes to grasp my waist. I spin on my heel, and step away from him. For my whole life, I've wanted to know who my father was.

Now I do. And he's the enemy of my fake-husband-fiancé. It's shattering. My mind explodes.

"Whatever he's done to you, we'll avenge," Thaxted says. "With me, you'll be the princess you were born to be."

"The only reason you got my daughter pregnant is because you came so early, you pathetic excuse for a dead-beat." Granny is really angry.

"Shut up!" he snarls and raises his hand.

"You think you can scare an old lady?" She shakes her head. "My daughter was better off without you."

"Richmond came after you to get to me," Thaxted says, sounding reasonable, moving away from Granny and towards me. "Because you're my daughter."

"Don't listen to that discount sperm bank reject," Granny says.

"Is this true?" I turn and ask Dom faintly. Why didn't he tell me?

"Taggie—" he begins, voice full of regret.

"Is it true?" I demand loudly.

Dom swallows.

"Just go, and live your life," Granny insists.

"He's been lying to you, Agatha," Thaxted says. "He's using you to get at me."

That can't be right. It can't.

"You're part of his pathetic revenge attempt. He seduced you. He's been manipulating you." Thaxted is smug now.

"No." Dom's single word is low and certain.

And maybe if my insecurities were a smidge more, I'd fall for this. What Thaxted is saying is so plausible. Except for one thing.

Dom stalked me, I already knew that. And yes, our marriage is fake.

But the seduction? Worst seduction ever.

There was nothing conniving in what Dom did, even if it was morally... Well. I'd say grey. But it's not. It's black.

Coming to my room. Jerking off. But it was me who pushed him further. It was me who lay, naked, and let him assume I was fast asleep. Who left my door open.

I invited him, because I wanted him. He's a mafia boss, and he told me not to leave my door unlocked. And I don't think without my encouragement we'd ever have gone further than sweet kisses in public and him satisfying his needs with his hand while I slept.

He's red flag bunting. But in his own fucked-up way, I believe that Dom was trying to be honourable. Trying to save me from his overpowering desire.

"You're a pawn in his game, Agatha," says Thaxted. "Don't you want to be an Essex princess?"

"Get out, Taggie," Granny sounds panicked now, pleading.

I don't think I'm a pawn to Dom.

Those nights... I'm not expendable to him. That sort of obsession isn't faked.

"You're my queen," Dom says softly. "He ignored you

for twenty years, Taggie. I couldn't stay away from you for even one night. You're my soul. My compass."

"A green flag to your red," I add, and reach out my hand.

Dom's takes it immediately, his eyebrows furrowed like he has no idea what I mean. Which, fair. He probably doesn't spend as much time watching videos on the internet as I do.

"Anything, Taggie," he says hoarsely and grips my fingers as though I might tumble into a ravine unless he keeps his grip on me. "I'll do anything."

"Then I'm staying with you," I say.

He holds my gaze for a long moment, and even though we haven't communicated as well as we should have until now, I see him understand. Enact the plan. He told me how he had Harrison in place in Thaxted's inner circle, and how he'd schemed to make Thaxted suffer losses to his family for years more, but that he'd give that up for me.

"You choose for your granny to die, then," Thaxted drawls as he strides over then reaches down to grasp Granny's hair, dragging her backwards.

"No!" I can't help but shriek, and lunge towards her instinctively. Granny cries out, but then goes silent, her face creased with pain.

Thaxted grins and shoves her away brutally, hitting the concrete since her hands are tied. "Better choice. Bring the girl to me."

The nearest of Thaxted's men makes a grab for my wrist, and I jerk backwards.

"Touch her and die." Dom's voice is dark and threatening, sending a shudder down my spine. I know how serious he is about that. I remember the blood.

Thaxted laughs. "You overestimate your power in this

situation, Richmond. You London boys always have. You don't have the stomach for mafia work, not really." He glances down with a sneer at Granny. "Coming to save a little old lady."

"I want you to know, Thaxted, before you die, who has been torturing you," says Dom calmly. "I've slaughtered all your children, bar one."

"What?" Thaxted blusters, but something flickers in his face. A slice of uncertainty.

"Kill him."

The young man at Thaxted's elbow steps forwards. A squeal of alarm emits from me like I'm a small furry animal in danger. But Harrison isn't making for me, or Granny.

It's a blur. A gunshot bursts and echoes in the warehouse, then more, and I'm pulled tight into Dom's chest.

Hiding is all I can do as terror rips through me, only stopping where Dom and I touch. I shake.

"Harrison isn't your son, he's my spy." Dom sneers as there's a watery gurgle. Blood, I realise. As Thaxted dies. "I already killed your last biological son, and your precious male lineage dies with you, Thaxted. The new leader of Thaxted works for me."

There's another choking sound, then hush apart from someone sobbing with fear.

"It's okay, it's okay," Dom says in a totally different voice. "I have you. I promised no one would ever hurt you again, and I meant it."

Me, I realise, as I remain tucked close to the man I love as he gives gruff orders. I'm crying. I clutch at Dom, not daring to look. "Granny?"

"I'm alive," my grandmother's voice rings out, sounding stronger than a woman who has been kidnapped has a right to.

Turning, I see Harrison helping her to her feet, her hands already freed.

"Granny." She's bruised, and shaking, but she raises her eyebrows archly. "This is the man who saved you, I suppose. Who you know from university."

I flush. Oh no. I'd forgotten about that. "I thought—"

"A pleasure to meet you, Mrs Hayes," Dom interjects, and offers his hand, keeping an arm around me. "I've been looking after your granddaughter, and I love her. We're going to get married as soon as the wedding can be planned."

"Hmm." She looks him up and down. "I suppose you'll do."

My mouth falls open.

"What?" Granny says, brushing off her top. "I think I can give him a chance, all things considered."

I look down at Thaxted, and the pool of blood oozing out onto the floor, then over at Harrison. "So that's it?"

"That's it." Dom strokes the hair out of my face lovingly and his eyes glimmer with a rich brown. "It's over. Time for a wedding and the happily ever after."

EPILOGUE
DOM

10 YEARS LATER

I still find nighttime a moment for indulgence.

I wake without a clear idea of why, and in the darkness, breathe in the sweet scent of my wife. She's cuddled into me, her back to my chest. Mia bambola.

Kissing her hair, I consider waking her. Or just using her in the dark until she wakes, as we both love. My cock sleepily begins to get interested.

A sound abruptly cuts off that idea.

It's a soft, plaintive cry. High-pitched, and sad. Our youngest son.

Dropping a kiss onto Taggie's shoulder, I slide backwards, then roll out of bed. Taggie murmurs a complaint in her sleep, and I tuck the covers around her to keep her warm.

Pulling on a pair of grey sweatpants and a T-shirt, I make my way to Alessio's room, next to ours, and look down at my wide-awake baby. In the glow of the nightlight, his dark eyes are the mirror of mine, and he waves his tiny fists up at me.

"Midnight treats, huh. It's a Richmond thing," I murmur, and reach down. Lifting him to lay on my chest. "You want some milk. Just as greedy as tuo Babbo." His dad.

The rest of our kids are as fluent in Italian as they are English, and I like to ensure they hear plenty of their grandmother's language.

Downstairs in the kitchen, I heat up his milk, holding him with one arm while doing everything with the other. After seven children, we have it down to a fine art, with a special milk warmer and bottles that turned out to be an excellent investment.

As we wait, I think through some of the mafia politics that have been bothering me, asking Alessio in Italian for his opinion. He cries a bit—getting fussy about waiting for his snack—when I mention Grant Lambeth, and I nod in agreement.

Yes. Entirely my feelings on the matter too.

I tell him he'll see his great-grandmother tomorrow. Taggie's grandmother still won't move in with us—fiercely independent—but she comes to visit her family several times a week.

When it's ready, I pull out his milk.

"You don't mind, do you?" I wink at my infant son as I take a sip. The milk is obscenely sweet, just like the woman who made it. And it's the perfect temperature. I screw on the teat and Alessio greedily sucks from the bottle. It's not long before he has a full belly, and his eyes are closing.

I lay him down into his cot, and he blinks up at me and smiles.

Fucking hell, Taggie and these creatures she makes.

They're all destined to ruin me and cause my heart to explode. So cute. So loveable.

Thankfully he slips off to sleep quickly, and I pad back to the bedroom Taggie and I share. She still has her own suite of rooms one floor up, and the kids have rooms on the same floor as us. There are nine bedrooms on this level, so one more to fill.

I'm looking forward to our last baby. We've been holding off, savouring the final time I'll breed her in truth.

I creep into bed and pull Taggie to me. She sleeps quite heavily, for a girl who stayed awake half the night when we first were together. She knows I have a taste for having her when she's asleep though, and sometimes...

But not tonight, unfortunately.

"You're awake," I rumble.

"How do you always know?" she complains.

I just do. "Taggie, you're my wife." I nuzzle her neck. She's warm and sweet and tempting. "I know, and love, everything about you."

EXTENDED EPILOGUE
DOM

I want.

That's the first feeling I have when I wake. I need. Desperately.

My cock is harder than stone and I am about to blow. And it's in soft, wet, warm heaven. The best thing I've ever felt.

Taggie. It's Taggie. I let out something between a growl and a moan.

My wife.

What is she doing? Torturing me, of course.

"Fuck. Mia bambola." She giggles around my cook, and the feel of it is an earthquake. She's amazing, my wife.

I don't take blow jobs from her very often, but when I do allow it, or she takes advantage as she has now, it's incredible. I'm flat on my back, my wife's mouth over my cock, helpless and at her mercy. There's nowhere I'd rather be, except perhaps between her legs. Maybe with my head there, or my cock. I'm not fussy. I do like to breed her, but pleasuring Taggie is almost as good.

She's moving over me, and I creep my eyes open. Our bedroom is full of pale pre-dawn light. Taggie is highlighted, her hair glinting, and her pink lips just visible under the cascade of her blonde curls.

The way she's bobbing up and down, so enthusiastic, so loving and giving, makes release surge in my balls.

She loves it when I take. She loves when I fuck her so hard she has bruises the next day. Says that she earned them.

It's a brutal treat even now when she wears my bruises on her body. I love those marks on her just as I enjoy her wearing my ring and my name.

"Taggie Richmond," I breathe, and reach down, tangling my fingers in her curls. "Bambola."

She speeds up, taking me deeper and faster and everything draws towards her.

My heart included. I swear it would beat right out of my chest, tearing me apart in its effort to get to her. I love her that much.

"I love you." Then I repeat the sentiment in Italian as she sucks me harder, her hand going to the base of my cock, while the other cradles my balls. Maybe it's something about her touch on that sensitive place, so knowing after ten years together, that sets me off.

I shoot into her mouth with no warning. It doesn't matter. She wouldn't have it anywhere else. My wife loves to have every drop for herself.

Coming with Taggie always catches me unawares with how intense it is. I'm struck dumb and paralysed. It's the pleasure of it, the waves of ecstasy, but it's more the sight of my wife with my cock in her mouth. She's unimaginably beautiful and hot.

Taggie keeps her lips over me as I come and come, throat choked with emotion.

I can't say anything. I'm her toy for once. My mind is totally blank. Just feelings, no thoughts at all. Is this how she felt, as I made her come all those years ago? Helpless in the best way, allowing me to be in control completely. I'm destroyed by her. Ruined, as though I wasn't already. I must have done something very good in a previous life to deserve someone as sweet and generous as Taggie.

With a growl, I drag her by the hair up to me, pulling so she's lying over my chest.

"Did you save it for me like a good girl?" I ask.

She nods.

"Give it to me then. Let me put that seed where it belongs."

Taggie blushes furiously. You'd think that after so long she'd be used to every kinky whim I have, but no. My girl still has moments of being sweet and innocent. She crawls further up my chest and leans down, bringing her mouth—hamster cheeked with come—to mine.

I open.

I remember spitting into her mouth for the first time so vividly. That need to be inside her was impossible to ignore, and it's just as strong now. Slowly, she presses her lips over mine and dribbles the salty liquid into my mouth. I stroke her hair and make a rumble of approval.

Then in a second I've flipped her over onto her back, and I'm on top of her.

She begins to open her thighs, but not fast enough, so I push them apart to reveal her glistening pussy. It always gives me savage satisfaction to see how she wants me. I pull her hips to a better angle and seal my mouth over her luscious pussy. I blow, forcing the liquid from my mouth into the only place it can go—up into her passage. She's still a bit gaped and empty from being thoroughly fucked last night, so some goes in, though admittedly, the second I take my mouth from her, it seeps out. I shift so I'm over her, fingers between her legs now and looking into her open eyes as I slide through the messy combination of both of our juices.

"Such a good girl for me," I croon. "But don't think that you'll get away without getting pregnant again, bambola."

She gasps.

My mouth finds hers and I kiss her deeply as I fuck her with my fingers, my thumb on her clit, and my other hand in her hair.

I push my tongue into her mouth, and the taste of her and me together is magic.

Even when she's making me more hers, she's mine. I plunder her and hold her soft little body to me. She's not as tiny as she was a decade ago, but she is still everything I could ever want. She always will be, however she looks when she gets older, however things change, as they inevitably will. There is simply an essence of Taggie that fits perfectly with me.

She writhes beneath me, and her hardened nipples rub on my chest.

"Dom!" She almost screams as she comes, and it's a good thing that the baby has his own room. The feel of her pulsing and clenching in waves has me groaning. I'll never be tired of her.

"Did you enjoy your wake-up call?" Taggie asks after she's recovered. A bit, at least.

I chuckle. "I did. Thank you, wife."

I roll us so I'm on my back and hold her to me, running my hands up and down her sides.

"What's happening today?" I ask, wanting to hear her voice more than I really need to know. Our joint calendar has all the details.

I twist her curls onto my finger as she lists out the various family activities. School for the older kids, and groups for the younger ones.

"Will you be able to stop work by five for Elena and Matteo's school play?" she checks anxiously.

"Of course." As though I'd forget our eldest kids' school play. I always make sure I'm there for the important events of their lives. I know Taggie still finds it surprising that I would put my family above all else, but she and the children are everything to me. My whole life.

To think that once, all I thought of was revenge.

"What are you thinking?" she asks when I don't say anything further.

I cuddle her even tighter. "That I'm happier than I could have ever dreamed."

THANKS

Thank you for reading, I hope you enjoyed it.

Want to read a little more Happily Ever After? Click to get exclusive epilogues and free stories! or head to Evie-RoseAuthor.com

If you have a moment, I'd really appreciate a review wherever you like to talk about books. Reviews, however brief, help readers find stories they'll love.

Love to get the news first? Follow me on your favored social media platform - I love to chat to readers and you get all the latest gossip.

If the newsletter is too much like commitment, I recommend following me on BookBub, where you'll just get new release notifications and deals.

amazon.com/author/evierose

bookbub.com/authors/evie-rose

instagram.com/evieroseauthor

tiktok.com/@EvieRoseAuthor

INSTALOVE BY EVIE ROSE

Grumpy Bosses

Older Hotter Grumpier

My billionaire boss catches me reading when I should be working.
And the punishment...?

Tall, Dark, and Grumpy

When my boss comes to fetch me from a bar, I'm expecting him to
go nuts that I'm drunk and described my fake boyfriend just like
him. But he demands marriage...

Silver Fox Grump

He was my teacher, and my first off-limits crush. Now he's my
stalker, and my boss.

Stalker Kingpins

Spoiled by my Stalker

From the moment we lock eyes, I'm his lucky girl... But there's a
price to pay

Kingpin's Baby

I beg the Kingpin for help... And he offers marriage.

Owned by her Enemy

I didn't expect the ruthless new kingpin—an older man, gorgeous
and hard—to extract such a price for a ceasefire: an arranged
marriage.

His Public Claim

My first time is sold to my brother's best friend

Accidentally Kidnapping the Mafia Boss

I might have kidnapped him, but the mafia boss isn't going to let me go.

Marrying the Boss

Baby Proposal

My boss walked in on me buying "magic juice" online... And now he's demanding to be my baby's daddy!

Groom Gamble

I accidentally gave my hot boss my list of requirements for a perfect husband: tall, gray eyes, nice smile, big d*ck. High sperm count.

London Mafia Bosses

Captured by the Mafia Boss

I might be an innocent runaway, but I'm at my friend's funeral to avenge her murder by the mafia boss: King.

Taken by the Kingpin

Tall, dark, older and dangerous, I shouldn't want him.

Stolen by the Mafia King

I didn't know he has been watching me all this time.

I had a plan to escape. Everything is going perfectly at my wedding rehearsal dinner until *he* turns up.

Caught by the Kingpin

The kingpin growls a warning that I shouldn't try his patience by attempting to escape.

There's no way I'm staying as his little prisoner.

Claimed by the Mobster

I'm in love with my ex-boyfriend's dad: a dangerous and powerful mafia boss twice my age.

Snatched by the Bratva

I have an excruciating crush on this man who comes into the coffee shop. Every day. He's older, gorgeous, perfectly dressed. He has a Russian accent and silver eyes.

Kidnapped by the Mafia Boss

I locked myself in the bathroom when my date pulled out a knife. Then a tall dark rescuer crashed through the door... and kidnapped me.

Held by the Bratva

"Who hurt you?"

Before I know it, my gorgeous neighbour has scooped me up into his arms and taken me to his penthouse. And he won't let me go.

Seized by the Mafia King

I'm kidnapped from my wedding

Abducted by the Mafia Don

"Touch her and die."

Filthy Scottish Kingpins

Forbidden Appeal

He's older and rich, and my teenage crush re-surfaces as I beg the former kingpin to help me escape a mafia arranged marriage. He stares at me like I'm a temptress he wants to banish, but we're snowed in at his Scottish castle.

Captive Desires

I was sent to kill him, but he's captured me, and I'm at his mercy. He says he'll let me go if I beg him to take his...

Eager Housewife

Her best friend's dad is advertising for a free use convenient housewife, and she's the perfect applicant.

Forbidden Employees

Kingpin's Nanny

My grumpy boss bought my whole evening as a camgirl!

Bratva's Secret Girl

She's my secret obsession. Then they find her.

Printed in Dunstable, United Kingdom